Christmas at the Harrington Park Hotel

From London, with love...

It's official! The Harrington Park Hotel is finally back in the hands of the family that founded it. And James, Sally and Hugo—the children of the hotel's late and great owner, Rupert—are determined to return it to its former glory. Just in time for the festive season!

But it's not just the Harrington Park Hotel that could do with a little holiday magic... It's the love lives of the Harrington siblings, who until now had drifted apart. This Christmas in Regent's Park, redemption and love might be closer than they think.

Discover Chloe and James's story in
Christmas Reunion in Paris by Liz Fielding

Read Edward and Sally's story in
Their Royal Baby Gift by Kandy Shepherd

And find out Erin and Hugo's story in
Stolen Kiss with Her Billionaire Boss by Susan Meier

All available now!

Dear Reader,

Harrington Park Hotel was a fixture in London in its day. But after decades of mismanagement and neglect, it stood in ruins until Hugo Harrington, son of the original owners, got the opportunity to buy it. He's a billionaire developer whose specialty is hotels because he grew up watching his dad turn Harrington Park into a one-of-a-kind experience for families—especially on Christmas Eve.

But fate's got some surprises in store for Hugo. First, he thought buying the hotel and involving his brother and sister in the renovations would reunite his family. He was wrong.

Second, he hadn't counted on falling in love with beautiful Erin Hunter, his event planner. He's sure he can handle all the drama and work surrounding the most important project of his life. But Erin's not sure the driven businessman is the right man for her, and Hugo's not sure he's the right man for anybody. It seems one of them is going to end up with a broken heart—while the fate of the hotel hangs in the balance.

I hope you enjoy Hugo and Erin's unexpected, unpredictable journey to finding real love.

Susan Meier

Stolen Kiss with Her Billionaire Boss

Susan Meier

Special thanks and acknowledgment are given to
Susan Meier for her contribution to the
Christmas at the Harrington Park Hotel miniseries.

Recycling programs
for this product may
not exist in your area.

ISBN-13: 978-1-335-55654-7

Stolen Kiss with Her Billionaire Boss

This edition published by arrangement with Harlequin Books S.A.

For questions and comments about the quality of this book,
please contact us at CustomerService@Harlequin.com.

Harlequin Enterprises ULC
22 Adelaide St. West, 40th Floor
Toronto, Ontario M5H 4E3, Canada
www.Harlequin.com

Printed in U.S.A.

Susan Meier is the author of over fifty books for Harlequin. *The Tycoon's Secret Daughter* was a Romance Writers of America RITA® Award finalist, and *Nanny for the Millionaire's Twins* won the Book Buyers Best Award and was a finalist in the National Readers' Choice Awards. Susan is married and has three children. One of eleven children herself, she loves to write about the complexity of families and totally believes in the power of love.

Visit the Author Profile page
at Harlequin.com for more titles.

To my dad, who loved Christmas Eve. He's the model I used to create Hugo, James and Sally's dad, who always made Christmas Eve special.

With abundant thanks to Liz Fielding and Kandy Shepard... So fun to work with you ladies on these wonderful stories!

Praise for
Susan Meier

"Are you looking for that book that will fill your heart with a warm glow? Then look no farther than *Falling for the Pregnant Heiress*. Susan Meier has once again told a story of two people you believe are real...you will not want to miss. The ending will melt your heart."

—*Goodreads*

PROLOGUE

Late November

AT ITS HEART, betrayal was always personal. It plowed deep ruts in a man's soul and weakened him until he almost couldn't breathe.

Though only seventeen when his betrayal hit, Hugo Harrington had fought the emotions threatening to suffocate him. He'd been framed for the embezzling done by his stepfather, and his mother had taken the side of her new husband, who had ordered Hugo to leave their home.

He hadn't been given time to say goodbye to his younger brother and sister, twins. He'd been told to pack and go. Every year, he'd sent a Christmas card to his siblings. Every year, he'd had no response. It was as if he'd been erased. Forgotten.

Still, he'd refused to let his losses or the wounds from being cast aside destroy him. Recognizing that if he let himself wallow he'd live the rest of his life alone, in the muck and mire of grief—taking the blame for something he hadn't done—his brain had sharpened. Not to save himself, but because some losses were unacceptable. Some wrongs had to be avenged. Some wounds wouldn't heal without justice.

He'd waited seventeen years for the chance to take possession of London's Harrington Park Hotel, and with it the opportunity to extend an olive branch to his brother and sister, but it had finally arrived.

"Mr. Harrington…" The voice of his personal assistant entered his private office via the speaker of his phone.

He turned from the wall of glass that displayed a jaw-dropping view of the Manhattan skyline with buildings appearing to be so close he could reach out and touch them. The sense that he was standing on top of the world filled him. That bolstered him too. It hadn't been easy getting here. But just like his opportunity, *he* had also arrived.

"Yes, Victoria."

"Your ten o'clock appointment is here."

"Send her in."

He walked from the window to his desk but didn't sit. The door opened and Erin Hunter entered. Her straight red hair fell to her shoulders in a blunt cut that always reminded Hugo of her no-nonsense attitude about work. Her efficient navy-blue wool suit appealed to the buttoned-up businessman in him. He currently resided in Manhattan, but he was a Londoner, born and raised. Precise and driven, he'd surrounded himself with only the best.

Erin Hunter was the best.

"Good morning, Erin." He motioned to the chairs across from his desk. "Please have a seat."

She sat, primly angling her legs toward the back of the chair and crossing her ankles.

"I have a new project. Probably the most important project of my life."

Her eyebrows rose. But a prudent subcontractor of his hotel development firm, she didn't pounce at his first words. She waited.

"The property in question is old and in need of so many repairs that work will be nonstop. It's in London. Formerly family-owned—" He nearly choked on those words. He wouldn't explain that it was *his* family who had owned it. The horrible truth would come out in good time. Maybe in London, after they'd been at the hotel a few days, when the sting of it wouldn't be so sharp, so cutting. "It passed to the hands of an incompetent and fell into bankruptcy. I scooped it up for a song."

She smiled. She loved a good business deal as much as he did.

"I want the grand opening to occur on Christmas Eve."

At that her mouth dipped. He was telling her they had weeks, not months, as they usually had. Still, she'd always risen to every challenge.

"Christmas Eve? Four weeks from now?"

"Yes."

She might have risen to every other challenge, but today she pushed herself up off the chair. "I'm sorry, Mr. Harrington. I'm booked."

"Booked?" He stood too. It wasn't that he didn't realize she had other clients. He simply assumed the high fee he paid her always propelled him to the top of her job list.

"You're talking about me spending the next weeks in London." She shook her head, causing her curtain of shiny red hair to sway. "*Christmas* in London. It's not possible." To soften the blow, she smiled at him, a quick, professional, no-hard-feelings lift of her lips.

For the first time since he'd known her, he reacted to the fact that she was beautiful. He'd *noticed* before. But something about the spark in her eyes at refusing him shifted her from beautiful to stunning and caused an unexpected scramble of his pulse.

Ridiculous!

He took a quiet breath to clear his head. Hugo

Harrington didn't mix business with pleasure, and the crackle of heat that raced through his blood definitely signaled pleasure.

Had to be an aberration.

"What do you mean, not possible?"

She raised her hands. "I have things scheduled. It is the holiday season. Plus, you typically give me more lead time."

"There's a reason I didn't." A master at winning arguments and swaying decisions, he motioned for her to sit again. "The property became available suddenly. I put in a bid they couldn't refuse, paid cash, and voilà, it was mine. I didn't have lead time."

"Maybe a later grand opening date?"

He gaped at her. "No! In its heyday, the hotel was renowned for its elaborate Christmas Eve celebrations. That's the prime time for the grand opening. The best way to demonstrate that the hotel everyone remembers is back!"

And the perfect way to remind his brother and sister of their shared past. A way to soften everyone enough that they could have the kind of conversation needed to clear the air.

Her brow furrowed. "Maybe next Christmas Eve?"

The weird heat crackled through his blood again. It was almost as if he enjoyed her arguing with him.

Couldn't be. He loved haggling and bartering. But he never argued with subcontractors. *He paid them.* They did what he wanted.

He spoke logically and concisely, as he motioned for her to sit again because she hadn't taken the last cue. "This hotel is very important to me."

Once again, she didn't sit.

His nerves jangled with annoyance this time. "You could even say it's personal."

"I'm sorry." Regret filled her eyes. "But being away from New York at Christmastime doesn't work for me." She extended her hand to shake his. Baffled, he took it. "Thank you, though, for thinking of me for this opportunity."

With that she was out the door. He stood behind his desk, in front of the magnificent view of the Manhattan skyline, the proof that he was at the top of his game. Not someone to be refused.

He heard the elevator doors open, then close, and his flummoxed thoughts cleared. She'd regretted turning him down, but she had turned him down. What the hell could be so important that she'd refuse him?

He grabbed his overcoat from his private closet and strode past his assistant's desk. "Have my car downstairs when I reach the street."

"Yes, sir."

He pressed the elevator button and one of three sets of doors opened. He hoped to catch Erin in the lobby. If he didn't, he had his coat and could follow her wherever she walked on this cold late November day. If she walked too fast, he would have a car.

That's the kind of guy he was. His plans had plans and those plans had contingency plans.

He didn't lose. Especially not someone as important as Erin. She was the preeminent party planner in Manhattan, but he'd used her all over the United States. If anyone could bring to life his memories of Christmas Eve at the Harrington Park Hotel, it would be Erin.

He caught up to her at the curb. When she saw him suddenly beside her, her blue eyes widened.

"We never talked money."

She frowned. "There's no reason to. I'm booked."

"For a bunch of office Christmas parties?" He made a *pfft* noise. "What if I agree to pay three times your normal rate?"

A taxi pulled up. She walked over and opened the back door. "I'm sorry, Mr. Harrington. The timing doesn't work for me."

She got into the taxi and the blasted thing drove away. Hugo jumped into his limo. Though it sounded like something out of a bad movie, he said, "Follow that cab."

He expected Erin's car to stop in the business district. Maybe at one of the high-rises housing the offices of one of the clients for whom she'd be working in December. Instead, it kept going. It seemed as if they turned every few blocks, and after forty long minutes, including driving through a tunnel under the Hudson, Hugo found himself in Jersey City.

Jersey City?

The taxi stopped at a modest four-story building. Hugo instructed his driver to hang back until Erin made a move.

After enough time passed for her to pay for the ride, she exited the vehicle, ran up the front steps and disappeared inside. He jumped out of his car and raced after her. He didn't reach her in time, but saw the elevator stop on the third floor.

When it returned, he followed her up. The doors opened and he stepped out cautiously, glancing around like Dorothy in Oz. He didn't expect Munchkins to pop out at him. He'd simply never seen an office building like this with white doors with two-digit identifiers. These couldn't be businesses. The doors had to lead to…*apartments?*

He knocked on the first one. An elderly woman in a housecoat answered, confirming his suspicions. He winced. "Sorry, wrong flat."

She laughed. "Flat?"

Baffled that he'd forgotten to shift his British slang to Americanisms, he apologized again and moved to the next door. No one answered. He knocked on the third door and a little boy opened it. The kid couldn't have been more than three.

Hugo froze for a few seconds, then said, "Sorry. Wrong…apartment."

"Noah! What are you doing answering the door?" Erin stepped out of a kitchen area, drying her hands on a towel. When she saw him, her mouth dropped open.

Well, she could join the club. Now he didn't feel like Dorothy in Oz. He felt like a man who'd inadvertently overstepped some boundaries.

The little boy had Erin's coloring—red hair and blue eyes—but a totally different face and eye shape. The flat behind them was simple, including an old-fashioned floral sofa that sat in front of a big window with plain beige drapes, and a kitchen without modern cabinets or shiny granite countertops. The cupboards were stained oak from another era. God only knew the material of the countertops.

Confusion and disbelief battled. From her familiarity with the home, he assumed she lived here. But why? He paid her a small fortune.

And the child who had her coloring—

It couldn't be—

Could his top-performing, always-there-for-him, executive-level event planner be…a mum?

"Can I come in?"

She hesitated. Hugo couldn't tell if it was from embarrassment or annoyance with him. But he hated this feeling of not being in the know. He always investigated everyone in his employ thoroughly. But as a subcontractor, Erin wasn't really in his employ—

Still, he needed to know.

He raised his hands imploringly. "I feel like we didn't sufficiently discuss my project."

She walked to the little boy—Noah—and put her hands on his shoulders to shift him away from the door. "Sure. Come in. Would you like some coffee?"

"Yes. That would be great."

Hugo Harrington stepped inside Erin's apartment, shrugging out of his cashmere overcoat. Their dealings had always been so crisp and professional, she hadn't for even a minute thought he wouldn't accept her refusal of his latest project.

But here he was. In her little condo. Her gorgeous, sexy as sin, biggest client, who always looked better in a suit than anyone had a right to, was in her apartment.

Tall and broad-shouldered, with dark chestnut hair that gleamed in the light from her overly bright kitchen, and brooding gray eyes, he'd been the object of her fantasies for the two and a half years they'd worked together. She'd never said a word, never made a move, always kept things strictly professional between them because she wasn't ready for another man in her life, but it didn't hurt to look.

And, oh, he was fun to look at.

She stopped the shimmer of attraction that lit her nerve endings. Nothing would come of her being attracted to him. Because that was how she wanted it.

As she popped a one-cup pod into her coffee maker, her short, auburn-haired mom called up the hall that led to the bedrooms. "Erin? If you're home for the day, I'm going out to get in my walk."

Seeing Hugo, she stopped dead in her tracks. "Oh, hello."

"That's Hugo Harrington, Mom. Mr. Harrington, that's my mom, Marge Winters."

He faced her mom with his always proper smile. "It's a pleasure to meet you."

She almost rolled her eyes. She might be super attracted to him, but she'd seen the way he'd looked at her apartment, the disdain that became confusion as he took in her out-of-date furniture and the cramped quarters. The attraction hadn't ever been mutual, but now that he'd seen how she lived she wasn't even sure he'd keep her as a friend.

Though come to think of it, they weren't really friends either. Her other clients invited her to parties and dinners to discuss their projects. Hugo Harrington only did business in his office.

Which might be for the best considering how attractive she found him.

"Can Noah go on your walk, too?"

"Sure," her mom said, overly cheerful, because she knew Hugo Harrington didn't merely pay for their apartment; he was the biggest contributor to the money she'd been saving to expand her business, employ more people and hopefully make enough to buy a condo in Manhattan, closer to her work, something with sufficient space that all three of them could be comfortable.

In the thirty seconds it took to brew Hugo Harrington's coffee, Erin's mom slid Noah into a coat and pulled a knit cap over his red curls. Erin bent down, placed a smacking kiss on her son's cheek and watched them leave the apartment.

Then she faced Hugo Harrington. He might be gorgeous and the object of her fantasies, but as a businessman he was single-minded. She'd told him no. He would try to talk her out of it.

Walking into her living room area of the open–floor plan space, she handed him his cup of coffee and motioned for him to sit. "I'm not sure what part of my decision you felt left room for discussion. But there is no room."

He looked around at her meager home. "I offered you three times your rate."

And assumed she should have been eager for it.

"There's more to a life than money." That's why her expansion was basically a dream right now. Noah was the only part of her deceased husband she still had. He was her world. Not her career and certainly not money.

Hugo Harrington blinked as if the concept of there being more to life than money was completely foreign to him.

She stifled a sigh. "December is Christmas, discussions about Santa, buying gifts, teaching my son to be generous and kind…" She lowered herself to the sofa across from the armchair he'd chosen. "I can usually work around your schedule and still have time for my son…but not if I'm in London."

Hugo's confused expression shifted as comprehension dawned. The fact that she had to explain the excitement of Christmas to him reinforced all her beliefs about the real Hugo Harrington. He wasn't the romantic, sensual man who inhabited her daydreams. He was a hard-nosed businessman, a guy who didn't have time for family, who didn't understand the meaning of the word *family*, a man who lived to work.

Well, she didn't live to work. She *couldn't*. Her mom may have been able to move in with her to help care for Noah when Josh died, but it wasn't the same for her little boy as having a dad. Erin knew that she had to be both mother and father and she refused to abdicate that responsibility…the way Josh had.

She closed her eyes briefly, hating that she felt that way. After all, her late husband hadn't asked for the heart attack that had taken him.

Thoughts of Josh rippled through her, her despair over his death, the sense of betrayal that came when she learned he'd been sick for months and hadn't told her—but he *had* confided in a woman he'd worked with. She'd told Erin that Josh had believed he was saving her the heartache of knowing her husband was dying while she was pregnant.

But good as his intentions might have seemed, not only had he confided in another woman, proving she and Josh didn't have the deep, wonderful bond Erin had always believed, but also they rang hollow as she'd stood at his graveside, ready to have his baby, without the opportunity to say goodbye.

She could have cried with him. They could have absorbed the first waves of loss together. Made videos of him laughing for their son. Made videos of him teaching Noah the kind of things a father longs to share with his child—

"You don't have any other clients, do you?"

She forced herself back to the present, to her discussion with Hugo Harrington. Sexy man with a heart of stone. Maybe that's what had reminded her of Josh?

"It looks to me like you can't afford to lose me."

Not about to give up Christmas with Noah, she sat taller. "I have other clients. Especially in December."

"But not clients who pay you as much as I do. Scattered Christmas parties. Grand openings. Not clients who pay a fee over the norm."

She took a breath. Part of her wanted to bluff her way through. The other part didn't like lying or even hedging. Josh hadn't out-and-out lied, but he'd kept a secret that had leveled her. She would never, ever again lie, distort the facts or omit anything.

She would face the truth. Always.

"You *are* my biggest client."

"Then let me suggest a compromise."

She brightened with hope. "I could supervise the project from New York?"

He chuckled. "No. But I could fly your son and your mum to London with you."

Her breath stalled in her chest. The casual way he'd called her mom "mum" hit her oddly. He did not sound like always proper Hugo Harrington. For a few seconds, he was the man in her fantasies. Not a businessman. Not a keen negotiator. But just a guy.

A handsome guy with chestnut hair and intriguing gray eyes—

"You may not be able to take your son to see Macy's Santa, but we have Santa in London. And wonderful shops." He caught her gaze. "Think of it as an opportunity to show Noah a more diverse Christmas."

She blinked, trying to see the real Hugo Harrington—the businessman, not the guy who suddenly seemed family friendly—as his idea of her mom and Noah going with her to London tickled her brain and began to take hold.

"I won't put you up in a hotel. I'll find you a flat. A place you can decorate with a tree and garland. And I'll make sure you leave work in time to tuck your son into bed every night."

She stared at him. She knew she did a good job for him. So it wasn't outlandish that he'd want her for a project with a looming deadline. And showing her son more of the world than one little corner in New Jersey appealed to her on so many levels. Noah would see one of the most beautiful cities on the planet, experience new traditions. She could teach him to think wider, beyond himself—

It was a generous offer from a guy who normally wasn't this kind.

Skepticism rose. "I'd still get three times my usual fee?"

He frowned.

She smiled shrewdly. "You can't take back something you've already offered."

He rose. "Sure I can. This is a negotiation."

And the real Hugo Harrington was back.

"Yeah, well. The way I see it, I have to pay staff extra to compensate for the fact that I won't be around to supervise my bread-and-butter projects in Manhattan."

He caught her gaze. "And the way I see it, you're already getting paid for those projects. The money will simply shift from your profits to the employees who assume your tasks."

"Which just took away my incentive to go to London."

His frown returned.

"Do the deal," she said, confident that if he really wanted her, he'd pay.

He sighed. "You don't have me over a barrel."

"Wouldn't think of even considering that. I'm simply someone who knows how to hold her ground." Her smile grew. "Whether you want to admit it or not, you like this side of me because I negotiate some very good prices for food and decorations and fancy pastries for your parties. You simply don't appreciate that I've turned that skill on you."

He rolled his eyes. Took a breath. And suddenly the ordinary guy was back. In all the years she'd done business with Hugo Harrington, he'd never been as normal, as human, as he had been today. He certainly wasn't the romantic man in her dreams, but she could swear he had a beating heart.

He sighed and said, "All right. Three times your usual rate. Lodging in London for three."

"And airfare."

"And airfare."

She extended her hand to shake his. "We have a deal."

CHAPTER ONE

"I DON'T SEE why you can't just flirt a little bit."

Two weeks before Christmas Eve, Erin Hunter stuffed the reports she'd worked on the night before into her briefcase. Holding Erin's son, Noah, her mom stood behind her in the open-plan apartment Harrington Enterprises had rented for them.

"I mean, look at this place," Erin's mom continued, glancing around at the gray walls that were trimmed with shiny white wood that matched the white cabinets in the kitchen. Black-and-white geometric-print tiles separated the cooking space from the huge living room/dining room area, which had hardwood floors accented by bright blue-and-white-print rugs.

"Only someone who really likes you would go to the trouble of getting us such a lovely apartment." She shook her head. "And I saw the way you looked at him when he came to beg—and I'm accenting the word *beg* here—you to come to London. I swear you all but swooned. You can't tell me you aren't interested."

Erin had been ignoring comments like these from her mom since she'd heard they would be spending Christmas in London. But that last one? That about stopped her heart. All this time she'd believed she was hiding the stupid crush she had on Hugo Harrington. But what if she wasn't?

"I didn't swoon. If you remember correctly, he'd shocked me."

"Which was probably why your true feelings came out."

She shoved more papers into her briefcase. She almost said there were no true feelings. Because what she felt for Hugo Harrington was one-sided and wrong. But she'd made that vow never to lie. "It's all totally irrelevant."

"Why is it irrelevant? You've been alone over three years," her mom said, following Erin as she walked to get her coat. "It's time. Even if nothing comes of it, you should flirt with him, if only to get your mojo back."

"Mojo?" She gaped at her mom. "I never had mojo. I fell in love in college before I knew mojo was a thing. And Josh had been the sweetest, kindest man I'd ever met, yet look what he did to me."

Her mom's expression saddened. "Erin, you have to let that go."

"Let what go, Mom? The fact that he never told me he had cancer or the fact that he *had* confided in another woman?"

"A *coworker*. He confided in a coworker. And you should be glad he did. She knew he'd been having experimental treatments for his cancer. So when he had his heart attack, she knew what to tell the ambulance people. It was awful that he died, but at least she gave him a fighting chance."

"And in the end, it didn't matter. The treatments he'd agreed to had pushed his body too far and he died long before he should have. He didn't even get to meet his own child. If he'd talked to me, I wouldn't have let him try something so risky."

"Faced with mortality, people do all kinds of weird things. Besides, your Hugo probably isn't anything like Josh at all."

She slid into her coat. "He's not my Hugo." But that was the problem, and the reason her mom's comments were so troubling. If her mom had noticed her looking at Hugo Harrington oddly, she wasn't hiding her crush as well as she'd thought.

And she knew why. She was losing her grip on the bottom-line reason she shouldn't like him. Damn that stupid conversation where he'd shown her his nice side!

"I think he could be your Hugo," her mom singsonged, hoisting Noah higher on her hip.

Ignoring that, she asked, "Will you and Noah be okay today?"

"He loves it here. I told you about our walks."

"Yes. It's good to get him outside."

"Give me another two days and we'll totally know the neighborhood." Her mom gave her a quick once-over. "Are you sure you want to wear jeans and a T-shirt? Maybe you should go put on that expensive blue sweater I bought you for your birthday?"

"Wear my *only* nice sweater to a hotel that's a construction zone?" She laughed. "I need clothes I can throw in the washer when I get home at night."

Her mother sighed, clearly disappointed Erin wouldn't dress up for Hugo Harrington. "Okay, if you think that's best."

"I do." Just as she thought flirting with Hugo would be a disaster.

Mojo.

For the love of God. She did not need mojo. She needed to stop thinking about Hugo Harrington, as if he were a nice guy. He was a businessman. He'd brought her to London because he liked her work.

That was it.

She kissed Noah's cheek, then smiled at her mom. "I'll be back a little after seven tonight."

Noah said, "Bye."

Her mom said, "Bye."

And Erin stepped out into the hall, squeezing her eyes shut as the apartment door closed behind her. She wished her feelings about Hugo hadn't changed. The crush she'd had on a fantasy version of him had been fun. Now everything felt real. She could barely take notes in meetings with him because the sound of his voice gave her goose bumps.

Damn it!

All because he'd shown her an inkling of a nice guy.

It was stupid…weird…*wrong*.

On the bus ride to Regent's Park, she told herself the whole mess had to be an extension of jet lag or exhaustion after the hectic week of getting herself, her child and her mother settled across an ocean, followed by a week of nonstop work with Hugo, setting out his plans for the grand opening.

Entering the hotel, she walked past scaffolding set up on concrete floors. Every room, hall and office waited for new carpet, hardwood or tile. Because *everything* was so old and had been neglected for so long, it all needed replacing.

As much as it was none of her business and potentially trouble, she couldn't stop her mind from tiptoeing over into the question that had plagued her since she'd arrived in London and her feelings toward Hugo had—softened.

Why the hell does he care so much about this hotel?

Sure, it was fabulous with high ceilings, chandeliers and decorative carved column caps throughout the lobby, corridors and event rooms, but there were easier projects than this shabby hotel. Even the marquis with the name had rotted and fallen off. The place was a disaster.

After taking her briefcase to her office and removing her coat, she dodged ladders and workers on her way to see Hugo Harrington, her heart adding an extra beat or two of excitement. Not because she entertained as much as an inkling of a thought of acting on her growing attraction to him. And not even to ask him why he cared so much about this old hotel. She'd never be that forward, especially when the British in him seemed to be more pronounced in his own country.

No. She was searching for Hugo for something entirely mundane: a check.

After striding through what would eventually be a workstation for the general manager's assistant, she opened the door to the manager's office—where Hugo set up shop when he was at the hotel. *His* assistant worked across town in a huge office inhabited by the New York staff in charge of renovations, so protocol was to simply walk in.

The enormous room had probably been a showstopper in its day. Dusty velvet drapes covered huge windows that looked out over the back of the property. Cleaning and painting this room had been scheduled for last because it wasn't a space that guests would use or even see. That was why the old filing cabinets along the left wall had been brought here when their original office space came up in rotation for painting.

Unfortunately, the chair behind the big mahogany desk was empty.

She should have turned and left, but she'd given Hugo a voucher to sign the day before and she needed the resultant check. If she had to pull the signed voucher from his outbox and walk it to the office across town, that's what she'd do. Though it was freezing out, she had to have that check.

She headed toward the desk. Rifling through the outbox, she didn't find it. With a wince, she rounded the area to the chair and sat, intending to only look through the small mountain of paperwork that had accrued, but an open drawer caught her eye.

A newspaper sat faceup. The front page picture was of the hotel—*the hotel*, the very one she sat in—in all its glory.

Her month fell open. The place was gorgeous. She could understand why Hugo wanted to restore it to its former artistry—

She stopped dead as the headline glared at her.

Harrington Park Hotel...
Is even more failure on the horizon?

Harrington Park Hotel?
Harrington?
As in Hugo Harrington?

Her gaze jumped to the top of the paper. Dated two days before her arrival in London, the newspaper had been off the stands by the time she'd come to the hotel. And she hadn't interacted with any of the contractors working on repairs—

She'd been too busy settling her son and mother into the apartment Hugo had rented for her and getting instructions from him about the party.

She read the first few paragraphs, interested in the hotel's history, but also confused as to why Hugo *Harrington* had bought this hotel. A hotel bearing his name? Maybe once belonging to his family?

The full details of Hugo Harrington's disappearance from the family had never been made public.

Oh, damn. It had belonged to his family.

The rumor was that Hugo had rebelled when his mother signed Harrington Park over to his stepfather, expecting to inherit the hotel himself. At a time when the hotel needed him the most, he'd packed his bags and left his family to fend for themselves.

Not the caliber of businessman Rupert Harrington, Nick Wolfe had tried to maintain the hotel, especially its Christmas Eve traditions, but without the help of the oldest son, Nick's efforts had failed. Too busy building his empire, Hugo hadn't even returned when his mother died. But he hadn't been too busy to keep watch over the hotel and snap it up when the last owner fell into bankruptcy.

"What are you doing?"

Erin's heart about burst in her chest and her gaze flew up as Hugo entered his office.

She sprang from his desk chair. "Looking for the voucher I gave you yesterday."

She just barely managed to keep her voice from shaking. He'd scared her, but the newspaper article had done more damage. Her stupid crush had been snuffed out. Totally. Brutally. She should have known someone so work-focused wouldn't give a damn about anybody but himself—wouldn't give a damn about his *family*.

But his not returning for his mother's funeral? Because he wouldn't inherit his family's sole possession? That was hard-core petty.

She tried to stop the comparison between Hugo and Josh, but it rose in a tidal wave of anger. Both thought only of themselves. Neither cared about the feelings of those around him.

Those *closest* to him.

To have made the decision he had, Josh clearly hadn't known her at all. And now it appeared, after two and a half years of working together, she didn't know her boss at all.

"I need the check today."

"I'm sure it will be coming when my office sends their courier with the mail."

And that was another thing—

Why did he have her *here*, in a makeshift office, among the construction and noise? Why wasn't she in the space rented for his New York staff?

Was it because he didn't want her to know his family had owned the hotel he'd scooped up for a song?

Scooped up for a song!

If his family had retained any part of the hotel at all, their share of the sale would be next to nothing. Was that what he'd been so proud of? That he'd shortchanged his family?

The man was scum.

As she scrambled around his desk, to the front of it where an employee belonged, he glanced down into the open desk drawer and frowned.

Then looked up at her.

Their gazes met and held.

He knew she'd seen the newspaper.

She swallowed but didn't shift her eyes away. Let him yell at her. She now knew the truth.

Her unspoken revulsion washed over Hugo as he slowly took his seat. He'd expected the story of the hotel would be printed in the business section of legitimate press. He hadn't expected the tabloids to pick it up…or that their accusations would skim along his skin like lightning before a bad storm.

"Satisfy your curiosity?"

Her chin rose. "Enough to know you're pretty heartless."

Anyone in London could say that to him and he'd shrug and go on with his life. But Erin Hunter had been like a right-hand person to him. She'd played a major part in his recent successes. He'd believed she respected him. No. She *had* respected him.

And one unsanctioned tabloid story seemed to have totally changed her mind.

Anger bubbled again.

"You didn't even come back for your mother's funeral?"

He hadn't been told his mother had died. No one spared the thirty seconds of internet searching it would have taken to find him.

"I wasn't told about my mother's death, let alone her funeral." He slammed his hand on the desk. He had absolutely no idea why Erin's disgust hit him in the chest like a stab of betrayal, but it did.

He wanted to scream, *Get out*. Instead, he drew a slow, calming breath, one that quelled the rising anger, not just with Erin but with his brother and sister who seemed so cautious about him. He'd wanted a happy reunion. What he got were two supercareful siblings. Though Jay seemed to be coming around, his only hope of repairing his relationship with Sally was the Christmas Eve grand opening party.

And for that, he needed Erin.

"I'll phone my office and track down the check."

She primly said, "Thank you," turned on her heel and raced out of the room.

He cursed, squeezed his eyes shut, then went back to work. Or tried. Her blatant hatred haunted him. They'd worked together amicably for the past week, got so many details nailed down—

So what?

People he *loved* hated him and he had survived.

He always survived.

To hell with her. His goal was repairing his family.

He worked until his brain forgot Erin Hunter and completely focused on his plan to bring his family's hotel back to life. At a little after six that night, the sounds of hammers and saws still filling the high-ceiling spaces of the first floor, he left the hotel. Tired, he ambled out to his waiting limo in time to see Erin heading up the long sidewalk around the driveway to the street.

Confusion overcame his automatic burst of anger with her. "Where's she going?"

The driver holding the limo door for him snapped to attention. "Ms. Hunter?"

"Yes."

"Probably to a bus stop."

Hugo gaped at him. "How far away is the apartment my staff rented for her?"

His driver opened the door a little wider, a hint for him to get inside and get them both out of the cold. "I'm afraid I don't know, sir."

"Well, it looks like we're going to find out. Stop when we reach her."

The limo took the circular drive around the hotel to the entry to the main road, then stopped. Hugo lowered his window.

She might despise him, and his feelings for her might also be in the toilet, but he wouldn't let her walk when he'd promised her a nice stay in London. "It's too cold to walk."

She tugged the sides of her coat collar closer together. "I'm fine."

And there was her pride again. Misplaced for sure, but he'd never allow her close enough that she'd see just how wrong she was.

Still… He wouldn't let a single mum, trying to get home to her family, take the bus when he had a limo.

"Let me give you a ride."

Miss Pride looked about ready to refuse, but she sucked in a breath. "For the record, I'm sure Manhattan is much colder right now."

He laughed as he opened the car door and got out, offering her entry to the warm back seat.

She slid in. He slid in beside her. "And for the record, I'm not in any way, shape or form showing you a nice side of myself, so you won't hate me after what you read in that paper."

She sniffed.

"I don't care if you hate me. I don't care if anyone hates me."

She snorted. "No kidding."

"And if you think I'm trying to repair our relationship, we don't have one. Except professional."

She glanced at him.

He held her gaze. "To ruin that, you'd have to screw up the Christmas Eve grand opening. You're too good to do that. Otherwise, I wouldn't have wasted the money bringing you here."

She said nothing, just stared at him, and he felt immeasurably better. He'd rather she hated him for being an unfeeling businessman than for things he hadn't done.

He gestured to the driver. "Give Ronnie your address."

She did and then settled back on the seat with a long sigh.

"Rough day?"

"My boss is a taskmaster."

He chuckled, not sure why her disrespectful side amused him, except that it felt good to have their argument from the morning out of the way. Or maybe he liked that she was always honest with him?

"He may be a taskmaster. But his hotels are some of the best in the world."

With another sigh, Erin realized she had to give him that one. "True."

"And you're a big part of that."

The sincerity in his voice warmed her more than the limo's heaters. She didn't want to like him or hate him and was glad that he seemed to be taking them back to their original impersonal work relationship. "Thanks."

"You're welcome. I don't ever say it, but I always hope the fee I pay you shows you that I appreciate you."

Grateful to be back on neutral ground, she glanced at him. When their gazes met, something trickled down her spine. She immediately blamed her stupid attraction, but her brain wouldn't accept that because her crush was gone. It had been snuffed out when she'd read that newspaper article. This felt more like a connection of some sort.

She hauled in a long breath, telling herself that was ridiculous. Guys like Hugo Harrington didn't connect. He'd proved that with how he treated his family.

He looked away and they drove a few blocks in total silence before he said, "Are your son and mum settling in?"

She peered over at him. A personal question after that weird connection? Her brain tried to make the leap that maybe *he'd* noticed her crush on him and he was making a move, but her crush on him was dead. Frankly, she'd like to keep it that way.

Deciding he was only making conversation, she said, "Yes. Noah is thrilled. I've taken him a few places, but we haven't officially been sight-seeing yet. We're saving that for the weekend— closer to Christmas, when Santa will be out, and everything will be more real for him."

"Humph. That makes sense. Have you given any thought to the Christmas cookies I mentioned?"

Yep. He was only making simple conversation, which he easily brought back to work. No need to worry he'd seen her crush or was even trying to be friends. She was safe.

"The gingerbread men?"

He nodded.

"Found three recipes online. I gave them to Louis Joubert. He'll make all three. You can do the taste test to choose the one you want."

"Good."

They drove the rest of the way discussing the project. So many details that Erin's head began to spin. Now that she knew the hotel had belonged to his family during its heyday, his surety of what he wanted didn't surprise her. But her heart tugged when it occurred to her that he could be recreating his past.

The memory of Hugo asking about ginger-bread men popped into her brain. At the time, she'd held back a laugh, thinking that must have been one of his childhood favorites. But what if they'd actually been a big part of the Christmas Eve celebrations of the past? And what if it had been his mom, not the chef, who'd made them?

What if those had been the cookies he and his mom had set on a plate for Santa?

Emotion swamped her and the sense of connection rose again. It was almost as if she could see him as a child.

She shook her head to clear it, but realization also hit her. Now that she understood the hotel had once belonged to his family, she'd be making all sorts of connections like this—

And whether she wanted to or not, she'd be getting to know him.

Her breath stalled. She did not want to like him! He'd deserted his family—

But she didn't want to hate him either. That would make working together difficult. And the truth was it didn't matter what he'd done in the past with his family. She was a subcontractor. Someone who worked for him. She'd do her best to keep enough distance that even if she did learn things about him, it wouldn't matter.

He. Was. Her. Boss.

The limo pulled up to her building and Hugo slid out of the car, motioning for her to exit.

Finishing the work discussion, she said, "Tomorrow morning, I'll send Dave and Terry on a scouting mission in the attic. We may find old lamps or paintings. Things we can use to draw out the ambience of the hotel when it was popular. Honestly, I think everything you want will be easy to accomplish."

He winced. "Even getting my brother and sister to hang ornaments with me?"

She slid the strap of her purse farther up her shoulder. Guessing that must have been one of their family traditions, she wished she could promise that, if only from a professional standpoint. But she didn't know much about his brother and sister except that he'd abandoned them, and she wouldn't promise something she couldn't deliver. She certainly wouldn't blame them if they wanted no part of hanging ornaments with him, as if everything was peachy keen and hunky-dory.

"Let me touch base with them before I commit."

He gestured for her to walk up the sidewalk to the building, and she frowned.

"I want to see your quarters. I was under the impression they'd found you something nice and close to the hotel. Since they blew the close-to-the-hotel part, I need to see what they rented for you."

Surprised by his concern, she said, "It's fine."

"I promised you an opportunity to show your son a wonderful holiday. Part of that is having a good place to live."

The odd feeling of connection with him tightened her chest again, maybe because he sounded more like a friend than a boss. "We do have good living quarters. Actually, they're wonderful."

"Let me be the judge of that."

They ambled up to the three-story building, which reminded Erin of some of New York's brownstones. He opened the main door for her, and she turned to the right to enter the first apartment.

As she opened the door, Noah jumped off the sofa and ran to her. "Mom!"

She scooped him up, turning to Hugo. "See? Perfectly comfortable."

He glanced around at the gray walls, white kitchen cabinets and solid hardwood floor in the living room and said, "It is nice." Then he looked at Noah, his eyes lit and his lips lifted into a smile. "How do you like it?"

Noah turned his face into his mom's shoulder.

"He's just shy," Erin said, as more conflicting feelings rippled through her. She hadn't expected all-business Hugo Harrington to be interested in her child. Estranged from his family, he was even more of a lone wolf than she'd originally thought. But judging from his expression, Noah intrigued him.

Still, everybody liked her adorable son.

"That's okay. When he sees the Christmas gift I told Santa to bring him, he's going to love me."

The little boy's head slowly lifted from Erin's shoulder. "Santa brings presents."

"And he takes special orders from bosses of little kids' moms."

Her heart began to soften at his unexpected kindness, but she stopped it. She liked not having a crush on him. She might have been righteously indignant on behalf of his family, but it made working for him so much easier.

She could not let a few kind words drag her back. Not when she had evidence that he wasn't a nice guy.

She kissed Noah's cheek then slid him to the floor. "Go sit with Grandma a sec, and then we'll watch a Christmas movie before bed-time."

Noah obediently did as he was told.

"He's a great kid."

"Thanks. He's a sweetheart. Barely a ripple of badness when he hit the terrible twos."

Hugo laughed. Then he glanced around again. "I'm satisfied with your quarters." He walked to the door and she followed him, see-ing him out.

He turned to her, and their eyes met. Her blasted attraction tried to rise again. She re-minded herself he'd abandoned his family, told herself anything nice he said about Noah was because Noah was adorable, and her defenses returned.

"See you tomorrow."

She murmured, "See you tomorrow." And almost felt guilty that she now knew enough about him that her feelings couldn't simply be neutral. She was either wondering what it would be like to kiss him or sitting on the edge of totally disliking him.

Still, smart women did not mess around with guys who thought so little of their families. No matter how good-looking he was or how strong her curiosity about what it would be like to kiss him.

CHAPTER TWO

THE NEXT DAY, meeting with Erin as she quickly reported on the progress of the details of the Christmas Eve celebration, Hugo was in awe. She was every bit as shrewd as he was in getting her own way and every bit as tough of a negotiator.

But something had happened the night before. Every time he'd looked at her, a weird sensation had shuffled through him. At first, he'd taken it as a continuation of his surprise to discover her disrespectful remarks amused him. But the more he'd stood in her quarters, the more times their gazes linked, the more he noticed odd little things about her. Things he *liked*.

Sitting in front of his desk, notebook on her lap, pen in hand, glasses perched on her nose, she went on with their meeting, totally oblivious to his confusing thoughts.

"The Christmas trees are ordered. Even the huge one for the ballroom."

Taking in her simple blue T-shirt that outlined nice-sized breasts and her worn jeans, he told himself that it was okay to agree that she could wear work clothes in a dusty hotel that was being renovated. But the nice-sized breasts observation was one of those unexpected things again.

Not that she wasn't attractive. She was. Maybe too attractive.

Seeing she was waiting for a response, he said, "Great. The trees are very important to the overall scheme of things."

"I saw that. I got the general idea of the size for each one from the old photos you gave to the contractor recreating the rooms and lobby."

Her hair caught up in a ponytail was also cute. Though it was abundantly practical when working in a construction zone, he liked it. He also loved that she hadn't lost one iota of her stunning beauty when she quit wearing makeup. The dusty environment had probably forced that too. But it had made his breath catch to see her skin clean and shiny, her bright eyes every bit as luminous without shadows and liners or whatever it was women used to make themselves pretty.

She needed none of it.

And it was confusingly odd that he reacted to that too.

"I've been in the attic with Terry and Dave and we've uncovered a treasure trove of decorations."

All thoughts of how pretty she was fled at the mention of decorations. He sat up. "The originals?"

Her blue eyes shone with victory. "I'm not a hundred percent sure, but they've been up there a long time, as if put in storage when the hotel changed hands and never used after that. With your brother and sister both out of the country, I'm going to need you to come up to the attic to look at them. Because you're only in the hotel a few hours a day, I called your assistant and made an appointment with you for this afternoon at one."

He laughed. "You made an appointment with me?"

She peeked up at him again. "You're a busy man. I don't assume you'll be free. I knew we had too much to discuss to squeeze it in this morning, so I called your assistant."

Which was another thing that made her so successful. She left nothing to chance. He adored that about her.

Actually, he now liked a lot of things about her. Too many. Especially for a guy who didn't date—

No, that wasn't true. He dated a lot. He didn't

have relationships. Erin was a relationship kind of girl. He might not have known she had a child, but he knew she'd been married and was a widow.

A widow.

Not the kind of woman a man dated for fun.

His thoughts about how much he liked her fled in the wake of that reality and pulled him out of the haze of whatever the hell seemed to be happening to him when he looked at her. With his brain back on track, they finished the meeting and she left his office, her arms stacked with papers.

After shrugging into his overcoat, he walked out to his limo, but rather than step inside, he turned and glanced at the hotel again. He'd put Erin in Harrington Park, instead of with his staff, because he wanted her to get a feel for the building. As the renovations were completed, he'd wanted her to breathe in the ambience.

Now he wondered if it wasn't a good idea for them to be separated. He didn't normally feel attractions like this one. Having space between them worked.

That afternoon, Hugo was back at the hotel for the meeting Erin had set with him. He exited his limo under the portico and raced into the lobby of the building, happy to see most of the scaffolding was gone. Probably moved to another section of the hotel. That meant the lobby painting was done. Now the registration desk would be sanded and stained to match the one from decades ago. Soon lighting fixtures would be installed like the ones from when his parents owned the hotel. Flooring would be next. Then the custom drapes. Then area rugs. All things that would bring his past to life again.

When Erin met him in front of his office door, strange tingling feelings of delight washed over him. Because they were wrong, he convinced himself he wasn't happy to see her but happy to be going to the attic, hopefully confirming that all the beautiful ornaments really had been stored and could be shined and hung on this year's tree.

"Give me two minutes to put my briefcase on my desk."

"You can take off your overcoat too." She winced, but her smile ruined the feelings of contrition he was sure she aimed to display. "You should probably ditch your suit jacket as well."

He did more than that. He took off his suit coat, loosened his tie and rolled up the sleeves of his white shirt. He knew the attic would be dusty and should have thought of this himself.

"How's this?"

"Magnificent," she said as she led him to the elevator that took them to the top floor of the hotel and down the hall to the hidden stairway to the attic.

When she opened the door, his past twinkled at him.

He took the last few stairs into the room filled with cobwebs, dust and memories, and his heart chugged to a stop.

She'd had Terry and Dave string the lights along the beams of the roof so he could easily identify them. Heirloom ornaments were displayed on long tables she'd commandeered from the kitchen.

Memories assaulted him. Christmas memories. He shoved away the visions of the night his stepfather had kicked him out and his mother had stood by passively, her silence telling him more than her words ever could have. He focused instead on the childhood memories of waking up Christmas Eve morning, filled with excitement over that night's party. The visit from Santa. The laughter of his parents—his dad alive and so full of enthusiasm it rippled from their living quarters through the hotel lobby, down the halls, into the kitchen, the ballrooms, the guest rooms, filling everyone with unbridled joy.

There'd been secrets, like the one Christmas Eve when a powerful businessman stopped the dancing at the ball to propose to his longtime girlfriend, making every guest a part of his proposal. Everyone had laughed with joy and toasted with champagne. Or the time a guest had received word she was pregnant after a decade of trying. Everyone had cried with happiness for her.

Because guests had been repeat visitors. Year after year, they'd gotten to know each other, become like family.

He touched the ornaments. Bright reds, golds and greens to be put on a green tree with gold tinsel and a gold star, all of which accented the special ornaments he, his brother and his sister had put on the tree. A new one for every year.

The plan had been for the special family ornaments to eventually replace the red, gold and green decorations, and for the tree to be filled with only ornaments placed by the siblings—

Then their father had died.

He cleared his throat, let the sadness wash through him until it thinned out and disappeared. Then he glanced at Erin. "Yes. These are all for the tree. Only white lights, though. The red and green strands were for the doorways of the lobby. We'll need live garland. Especially for the main stairway."

He pointed at a box of all red ornaments. "Those decorate the garland on the banister."

He could see it. His dad bigger than life. His

mum always laughing, involving her children. The best mum in the world because she'd loved them—

He'd always believed she loved *him*.

He closed his eyes and took a breath hoping to stop the memories, but they seeped into his thoughts, into his psyche, like ghosts with nowhere to go, so they haunted his soul.

Holding on to his composure by a thread, he pointed at a box of green and gold. "And those go on garland hung on the reception desk."

She frowned. "Hmmm…it's not done. It's not even stained yet—"

Overcome with emotion, he turned on his heel and headed for the stairway. "It will be. It will all be ready on Christmas Eve."

He strode to his office, fighting the emptiness of missing his parents and the confusion of his last night with his mum, wishing his life had been different and longing to rebuild his relationship with his siblings. He'd been their older brother, their protector. And then suddenly he was nothing.

No one.

He sat behind his desk, still reeling from seeing the decorations, and closed his eyes. Not in despair, but in confusion. He knew seeing everything would bring back memories, but he'd genuinely believed he had gotten beyond his mother asking him to leave. He'd become a man, a success. Why did he care?

Two taps on his door forced his eyelids up, shoving him back to the present. "Come in."

The door opened and Erin gingerly stepped inside. "Are you okay?"

The very question raised his nerve endings like porcupine quills. He didn't like being weak, confused. Worse, he didn't want his staff to see it. "Of course, I'm okay."

"Mr. Harrington—Hugo—I've seen you angry, and though you scared Terry and Dave when you stormed out of the attic, that wasn't anger."

He sat back, took a slow breath. "Didn't fool you, huh?"

She ventured a few more steps into the room. "It was close. And then I asked myself who gets angry over gorgeous antique ornaments? No one."

"So, you answered yourself?"

"If you're trying to make me think I'm crazy for talking to myself, that's not going to work either." She took another two steps. "Something's very wrong here. And I'm worried that I'm going to spend the next two weeks creating a wonderful event only to have you ruin it."

"Me?" He gaped at her. "Ruin it?" He pointed at his chest. "*I'm* going to ruin it?"

"I know when something's bubbling under the surface."

Only one of his eyebrows rose.

She huffed out a breath. "Seriously, you dragged me to London for a project that's almost too big to pull off. *You're* a bundle of nerves. And the press is watching you. Which will mean if you snap and the big Christmas Eve grand opening fails... Guess whose name will be ruined in London and probably Manhattan because you're such a hot item all over the globe?"

He said nothing.

"I don't fail, Hugo. If you're pushing to prove something, that's a recipe for disaster and I want no part of it."

"I'm not pushing to prove something." He sat back. "And I won't snap."

"Says every person right before they snap."

He would have laughed except he could see in her eyes that she was serious. He also knew why. She had a child to support. If this failed and her business suffered, her income would nosedive.

He tried to envision anyone else capable of accomplishing the grand opening celebration he wanted and knew there was no one else. They had not quite two weeks left, and she was knee-deep in the details. He couldn't bring in another person. He had to keep her.

He also had to make sure she didn't fail. He'd never forgive himself if he took food out of the mouth of a child. He'd been hungry one too many times himself in those weeks after he'd been kicked out. He knew that anguish just a little too well.

He rose and walked to the closet, where he grabbed his jacket and his overcoat. "All right. You're right. I *am* tense. But I probably just need a release valve." He didn't exactly want to talk, but if he did, what better person to vent to than someone he only saw every few months? Not even an employee, but a *subcontractor*. Someone who had more reason to keep his secrets than spill them.

"But not here." If he did let loose, he didn't want anyone to overhear. "Have you been sight-seeing yet?"

She frowned at him. "I'm at the hotel twelve hours a day. Home in time to put Noah to bed, as you promised. But not home in time to sight-see."

"Do you like hot cocoa?"

"Everyone likes hot cocoa."

"Get your coat and meet me outside. I'll show you the one place you're going to want to be sure to take your son."

They rode in his limo to the Southbank. It wasn't a long trip, but it was long enough that

Erin about broke her neck, her head moving from side to side, as she tried to take it all in.

He laughed, and for the first time since he'd been to the attic, some of his tension released. "London has a lot to see."

"I know." She smiled at him. "I can't wait."

More of his tension abated. "It's a beautiful city."

The car let them off and he pointed out Westminster Bridge and Big Ben as they began their walk along the Thames.

She gasped. "There is no feeling to describe being places that you thought you'd only see in pictures. It's surreal! Almost like I can't believe I'm here."

He glanced at the bridge, then Big Ben again, viewing both with fresh eyes. "I guess you're right." He breathed in the crisp air—Christmas air. He could suddenly feel the holiday coming to life around him, overriding his memories.

More of his tension ebbed. His head cleared. *Maybe he'd just needed some fresh air?*

When they reached the Beltane&Pop van, he directed her to look at the flavors and asked what she wanted.

Her mouth opened in surprise and finally she laughed. "You know what? Just plain old hot cocoa."

He ordered two and they began their walk

again in the crisp air. The sun was bright, but dark clouds eased in. Soon snow would be falling.

She took a sip and groaned. "This is fabulous."

Calm settled over him, along with the unexpected sense that he was happy to be out of the office, a sure sign of overwork, not overwhelm. Meaning, he was fine. "We like to think it's the best in the world."

Her head tilted as she turned to look at him. "That's the first time you've ever referred to London in a way that makes me think it's your home."

"You saw the newspaper article. I didn't leave on the best of terms."

"Is that what's bothering you?"

He shrugged, took a sip of his own hot cocoa and said, "Honestly? I think I've been pushing too hard and it all came to the surface this afternoon."

"That's interesting because I thought maybe you were trying to recreate something you worry can't be recreated."

Her comment hit him right in the heart. He'd never verbalized it to himself, but deep down that was his fear. Not merely because his father was the engine of their joyous Christmas Eve celebrations, but because his brother seemed to have accepted his return only grudgingly, and his sister clearly hated him.

But as much as he trusted Erin, he wouldn't tell her that. He'd stick with his story that he'd been working too hard. Because coming outside had proved it to be true. The walk had cleared his head, and he wasn't noticing those odd things about Erin—

Which was the real reason it would be incredibly foolish to confide in her. He liked her. And she wasn't right for him. Or maybe he wasn't right for her. A woman with a child needed a relationship, not a one-night stand. And he was Mr. One-Night Stand.

"Yes and no." He peeked at her. "The project is ambitious and tied to some memories. It would be wonderful to recreate them, but I know there are things that I can't get exactly right. So, I only need to get close to what we had." He took a breath, then smiled. "When have you ever known me to fail?"

Erin studied the confident expression on his face. Whatever had upset him, it was gone. Or tucked away to pop out when they least needed it? Like the day of the grand opening?

"Come on. You said you wanted to talk."

"No. You said I *needed* to talk. But I don't.

I'm fine. You saw the newspaper article. I'm heartless."

Before the trip to the attic she had believed that. But watching his happiness at seeing the family ornaments morph into something deep and profound, something that looked like amazement colored with sadness, she wasn't so sure.

Here they were, at a crossroads, a place where he could talk, confide a fact or two or keep everything bottled up, and he picked silence.

She took another sip of the perfect hot cocoa as they walked into a market dedicated to Christmas. Light and color winked at her. Part of her simply wanted to enjoy the break. To let him be the stubborn man he always was.

The other part—the part that knew this could blow up in their faces—tried one more time. "I don't think you're heartless."

"What? You mean all that anger you had for me after reading the article about the hotel was fake?"

Her face reddened. "It's the first personal thing I'd ever read about you."

"And you chose to believe it. Out of hand. No other facts at your disposal, after working with me for two and a half years, you chose to believe it."

"It's not like I really stopped and made a choice—"

"No kidding." He turned around. "We have our cocoa and you know to bring your son here on your sightseeing day. Plus, we both have tons of work." He smiled but the sentiment didn't reach his eyes. "It's time we got back."

He started walking without waiting to see if she'd follow him.

She did, of course. He was her most important client and her ride back to the hotel.

But regret and something else followed her to the waiting limo, as the wind kicked up and the once-blue sky quickly darkened. There was absolutely no reason in the world why a successful, important guy like Hugo Harrington would care what she thought of him. But she cared about her own behavior. And he was right. After enjoying working for him for two and a half years, she shouldn't have let one article sway her opinion of him.

Of course, her original thoughts about him hadn't exactly been flattering, either. She believed him to be a hard worker, but a taskmaster. A *gorgeous* taskmaster, but still a taskmaster. Though she would let him light up any fantasy, even she admitted she wouldn't want him in real life.

That seemed so horribly wrong. The flashes of kindness she saw in him almost demanded she admit that something was out of sync in his life. And if she wanted to make sure they pulled off the grand and glorious Christmas Eve reopening celebration he'd planned, she might need to know what it was to make sure they didn't fail.

She almost winced. Did she really want to know a guy who'd set the world on fire professionally but had a huge rift with his family?

If it got the project done right—and on time—and to accolades, not condemnation, then, yeah. She was going to have to get to know the real Hugo Harrington enough that she could keep a lid on whatever emotion had almost pushed him over the edge that afternoon.

CHAPTER THREE

A LITTLE AFTER SIX, Hugo texted his driver, ready to go to his flat on the other side of town. Then he texted Erin, telling her she could ride home with him. The afternoon's darkening clouds had unleashed wet snow that turned into thick white flakes that now fell in earnest. Hugo wouldn't force her to wait for a bus when he had a limo at his disposal.

Erin sent him a text thanking him and telling him she was in the attic and would be down soon.

He told her that was no problem as his driver hadn't arrived, then waited another five minutes before he texted Ronnie again.

No answer.

After twenty minutes, he finally got a text informing him that roads had closed. As Hugo had sat in his office working that afternoon, six inches of snow had fallen. Ronnie had spent the time since his last text checking all the routes out of the city. He was sorry but Hugo was stuck at the hotel that night.

He texted back.

No problem. The top floor penthouse suite is ready for guests.

Plus…he had work. He always had work.

For some reason that didn't sit right. It should have made him happy to know he'd be busy. Instead, discontent shimmered through him.

Ronnie bade him good-night. He promised to keep a watch on the condition of the roads and be at the hotel as soon as he could the next morning to take Hugo to the office set up for his Manhattan staff.

Hugo thanked him and rose from his seat. After opening the drapes behind the desk to watch the snow pouring down, he stretched the kinks out of his back.

The office door burst open. "Hey. Sorry, I took longer than a few minutes, I—"

Erin stopped abruptly, staring at him as he stretched. Her eyes wide. A breathy gasp escaping.

Tingles rippled through him, setting a little fire in his blood. He ignored it. He'd forgotten her when he'd so easily told Ronnie it was no problem for him to stay at the hotel. No matter.

Erin wasn't going anywhere either. Plus, there were two master suites in the penthouse. He and Erin might be attracted, but he'd already decided not to do anything about it.

"I think I'm the one who has to say sorry. I knew it was snowing but forgot to check on road conditions. My driver can't find a way to get here to pick us up or take us home."

She ventured a little farther into the room. "Even buses aren't running?"

"Ronnie tells me they've closed the roads. It's all good, though, because the top floor of the hotel is a penthouse. There's a little kitchen, a huge sitting room and two bedrooms that are suites." He accented the word *two*. "The place didn't need much repair work, mostly just cleaning. It was done first so I could use it the weeks before I bought my London flat. I'll bet the bar is even stocked."

She stared at him.

He opened his hands in supplication. "Come on. I'm sorry. Really, I've been up to my neck in work. Normal things like snow and bad roads don't always register on my radar."

She took a breath. "That's okay. In all fairness, I didn't notice it either. Give me two minutes to call my mom and say good-night to Noah and I'm all yours."

His blood surged when she said she would be

all his. He scolded himself as he reached for his jacket and overcoat while she stood in the hall, talking to her mum and son.

Her call complete, she turned to face him with a smile that about knocked his socks off. Oh, this was dangerous. She was beautiful and smart and everything he looked for in a woman—

To sleep with.

He didn't do relationships. And she needed a relationship.

That reminder firmly in place, he headed toward the door and she smiled again, sending another whoosh of sexual energy through him. Enough voltage that his conclusion waivered.

Was he really sure she needed a relationship? Just because she'd been in a marriage and had a child, that didn't mean she didn't like fun—

Did it?

Good grief! What was wrong with him that he couldn't stop thinking about sleeping with her?

Once again, he reminded himself that she wasn't someone to trifle with. Especially when he needed her. She might not technically be an employee, but she was still working for him.

They rode to the top floor in silence. The doors parted and he motioned for her to step out into the open—floor plan room. A small white-and-marble kitchen sat to the left. A navy-blue-and-sage sitting area took up most of the available space with sofas, chairs, area rugs, a bar and even a piano. Two white doors in the back led to the sleeping suites.

"See? It's big. Plenty of room for both of us." He pointed at the doors. "And two bedrooms."

All right, maybe he'd said that a little too emphatically, making his voice squeak and himself sound like he wasn't as calm and casual about them staying the night as he should be.

Pulling himself together, he strode to the sitting room wet bar that fronted the windows in the back. He pulled out a bottle of bourbon. "Bar's been stocked."

She ventured another step or two inside.

He headed to the kitchen, marched to the refrigerator and swung open the door with relish, ready to show her a stocked fridge. Unfortunately, it was empty.

"Oh."

She finished the walk to the center island. "Actually, we don't have to worry about food." She pulled a plastic bag of grapes and one of cheese out of her briefcase.

He frowned. "I am not a woodland creature who can survive on grapes and cheese."

"Now, don't be snooty." She rummaged in her briefcase again and pulled out another container. This one looked like a lunch sack made of a happy floral print.

"There are two sandwiches in here."

He gaped at her small form. "You eat two sandwiches for lunch?"

"No. Usually I eat one for lunch and one around six at night." She peeked at him sheepishly. "That's when I get hungry. So that's my dinner. I don't wait to go home to eat."

He crossed his arms on his chest. "A sandwich is your dinner?"

"Yes."

"Every day?"

"Yes."

"Is that really healthy?"

Her eyes narrowed. "Look. Are you hungry or not?"

"I guess it depends on what the sandwiches are."

"Turkey and mustard."

Surprise made him smile. "I like turkey and mustard."

"Then you are in luck. Add a few grapes and some cheese and you have dinner."

He slid out of his jacket and took the sandwich she handed him. "Why didn't you eat lunch today?"

"Busy. Later, when we went for our drive, the hot cocoa filled me up."

He remembered their time in the attic. Remembered that she'd more or less talked him down from the ledge when ghosts of Christmas Eves past filled him with sadness and questions. And though he hadn't confided in her, getting out of the office had certainly helped him regain his equilibrium.

"That was good hot chocolate."

"It was," she agreed, then took a seat at the kitchen island that served as a breakfast bar.

He sat beside her. She opened the bag of grapes and the bag of cheese, setting each in the center, an invitation for him to help himself.

He felt odd having Erin share her last food with him. Not that he thought they would be stuck in the hotel for days without sustenance. It was the kindness of the gesture that struck him.

Usually, people didn't care about him. Oh, his driver asked him if he wanted to stop for dinner every night or coffee every morning, but that was more of a logistics thing. Ronnie needed to know if he'd have to pull over at a coffee shop or restaurant.

Erin sharing her food was pure kindness, a gesture that reached into his chest and softened his heart, even as it made him warm all over, made him want to be close to her—

He jumped off his chair. "How about a drink?"

She sniffed a laugh. "What?"

"The bar fridge is stocked with beer and mixers. I'm not a bartender but I can look up anything you want and make it." He smiled. "How hard could it be?"

"I guess not too hard." She licked her lips. "You know, it's been a while since I had a drink. I'm not even sure what I'd like."

"There are various martinis that are popular."

"No. I'm not a fan of hard liquor." Her face brightened. "You know what I want? A glass of wine."

"White or red?"

She giggled. "I can't believe I'm having a drink."

"Well, you don't have to be awake or alert for your son tonight. So, if I were you, I'd take advantage."

"Okay, then I'll have a glass of white."

He brought the bottle to the kitchen island along with two glasses, poured one for each of them and handed the first to her.

She sipped cautiously, then savored. "Anyone who says kids don't really change your life is lying."

He burst out laughing. "I don't think anyone's ever said that."

"Good, because it would be a lie."

The warmth of companionship swelled. That

subtle feeling of total relief at being with someone you don't have to put on airs for.

Oh, Lord.

He really liked her.

Which was why he wanted more. He did like
her. And they had a whole night—

The thought filled him with longing for things
that went far beyond sex. Something he'd never
felt before.

He ignored it. If he'd never experienced it
before it had to be wrong. Plus, he could be
friendly and withstand an attraction.

Couldn't he?

Their gazes caught and his chest expanded.
Part of him wondered why he was fighting this.
The other part simply couldn't get enough of
looking at her.

That was the part that seemed to be taking
control.

And he wondered again why he was fighting this.

When their sandwiches were gone and their second glass of wine was almost a memory, Hugo
picked up the bottle and directed them to the
sofa. Erin couldn't believe her luck in getting
to spend time alone with him. To keep this project from imploding, she needed to get to know
him. Needed to understand whatever it was that

might cause him to snap. He was softening to her and any minute now she expected him to start confiding.

He refilled their wineglasses and sat beside her. Not close. But not far enough away either. She could smell his aftershave and see every muscle move beneath his white shirt.

Not that she was looking.

Oh, hell, who was she kidding? She *was* looking. Being stuck together and having the best-tasting wine on the planet had softened her. Maybe even lowered her inhibitions. If she hadn't been spending time with him for such a good cause—getting to know him, hoping to discover his secret so it didn't tumble out at the wrong time and ruin their grand reopening— she'd be scrambling out of here. At least, excusing herself to go to her room, away from the hypnotic power of those beautiful gray eyes.

But wouldn't that be a waste? They had a bottle of delicious wine. He was chitchatting like a friend. For the first time since she'd had Noah, she was having fun.

Fun.

With grouchy pants Hugo Harrington.

She laughed at her Noah-age reference.

"What's funny?"

Caught, she remembered her no-lie rule and said, "Something popped into my head."

He smiled at her. Simply. Beautifully. "What?"

She swallowed. It had to be the wine, but he was behaving like the man in her dreams. "Something Noah says when my mom's having a bad day."

His smile warmed, grew.

She cleared her throat. Lord, he was gorgeous. And so muscled and male. She swore she felt heat radiating from him.

"Is it hot in here?"

He laughed. "Actually, yes."

"Whew, because I'm definitely feeling warm."

He slowly caught her gaze. "Top floor. Heat rises. I could turn on the air conditioning."

He was only being considerate, but her chest tightened. Her mouth watered. Visions of things that had never really happened filled her head. Could things she'd imagined doing with him for so long actually be coming true? Her breath caught.

She shook her head slightly. Thinking of those things—those fantasies right now—really, really wasn't smart.

But something pulsed between them. With their gazes locked, he leaned in and brushed his lips across hers. Her heart fluttered. The wineglass between her fingers slipped a notch.

He caught it and set it on the coffee table in

front of the sofa, along with his glass. Then he leaned in again. One hand on the back of the sofa, the other at his side, he slid his lips across hers again.

Arousal hit in a wave of longing so strong it made her bold. She slid one hand to his shoulder. He slid his hand to her waist, tugging her closer. His mouth moved over hers seductively, drawing her in, and she fell into the kiss, exactly as he lured her to with his clever mouth. Her other hand moved to his shoulder, and this time she was the one to pull him closer.

The kiss changed, deepened. With just enough wine to lower her inhibitions, she let her fantasies meld with reality and tumbled into the warmth surrounding them. Adrenaline competed with arousal for control. When his fingers went to the hem of her T-shirt, anticipation raced through her, and she shifted so he could pull it over her head. He tossed it behind him.

His palm met the soft flesh of her belly, and her blood tingled. When his smooth fingers slid beneath the lace of her yellow bra, it jumped to boiling. Glad she'd worn the pretty bra, she reached behind her to unhook it. As she slipped it off, Hugo rose and took off his shirt. Without giving either of them time to think, he lowered himself to the sofa again, this time on top of her, his thigh between her legs as their bare chests met.

Emotions rushed through her. She wanted to touch him everywhere at once, but slowed her pace, memorizing the feel of his solid skin and those wonderful muscles beneath her hands. He ran his lips along her arms, her shoulders, her chest until he reached her breasts.

From there everything became the frantic motion of two desperate lovers. She knew her excuse. It had been years since she'd been with a man. But she doubted the great Hugo Harrington went years without company.

His desperation would have confused her except their joining was probably the most perfect physical thing she'd ever experienced, and she didn't let confusion or questions mar it.

When they reached the end, she lay beneath him, sated and dumbfounded. Not just from the pleasure, but because she'd never done anything like this…and with her boss?

She waited for embarrassment or regret. None came.

"You okay?"

She looked up into his smoky gray eyes and smiled. "Honest to Pete, I don't think I have ever been better."

He laughed and she felt the rich rumble in his

chest against hers. "That's exactly what a guy likes to hear."

He levered himself to sit beside her, then held out his hand to help her sit.

When they were side by side, he quietly said, "I don't usually lose control like that." He ran his hand along the back of his neck. "But I'm glad I did. That was pretty amazing for me too."

Pride fluttered through Erin. Dumbfounded that she'd so thoroughly pleased him, she had no idea what to say.

He shrugged into his shirt before grabbing the wine bottle. "We could fumble our way through excuses and say it won't happen again because tomorrow we have to work together, and it probably shouldn't happen again. But we still have the rest of tonight. We could go back there." He pointed at the last door. "And not worry about tomorrow until tomorrow."

Part of her knew the next day probably would be awkward. The other part realized this was a once in a lifetime opportunity. A chance for a fantasy to play itself out. A chance to just be a woman, not an ambitious business owner, not a daughter helping support her mom, not the mother of a feisty three-year-old. Thanks to a blanket of snow, she could simply be a woman for a few more hours.

With the sexiest man she'd ever met.

He bent and cruised his lips along her neck.

Oh, yeah. She wasn't letting this chance get away.

She woke nestled into his side and her heart swelled. He was perfect. He'd shown her another side of himself the night before. A sexy side, a demanding side—mixed with unexpected softness. He'd touched her with a reverence that stole her breath and made her wonder—

Was there more to Hugo Harrington than a guy driven to succeed? When she added their night together to his emotion when he'd seen the decorations in the attic, she knew that deep down he was a normal guy. And she wondered if she'd only seen his harder, secretive side because that's all he showed his employees.

"Good morning."

His words tiptoed across the pillows to her.

Here it was. The moment of truth. She wished he would be sexy, sweet Hugo. But the night before he basically told her there would only be one night—

He raised himself up and onto his side, then ran his lips across hers in a soft kiss that melted her heart. But he quickly pulled back, turned away from her and grabbed his phone from the bedside table.

"Roads are cleared."

Her heart sambaed. Sweet, sexy Hugo was gone.

A wish that things could be different tried to form but she stopped it. He'd spelled things out after the first time they'd made love. But she'd wanted her fantasy lover. And she'd gotten him. The fact that he'd been better in reality than he had in her daydreams didn't change who he was: cool, aloof Hugo Harrington, keeping the nice guy side of himself hidden, probably because he was a man with secrets.

Still.

He hadn't told her one personal thing the night before.

"You can go home and change, if you want." He didn't look up from his phone. "I won't tell your boss."

A thousand emotions sparred in her brain. Everything about the guy he'd been the night before had been perfect. But she also knew she'd never get involved with another man with secrets, another man who didn't understand intimacy. A man who only let the nice guy out when he needed or wanted something.

She swallowed. "I think I'll be okay in my clothes from yesterday, after I get a shower."

Damn her voice for stuttering with confusion.

He set his phone down with a sigh. "Sorry if

I seem grouchy to you. I'm not in the habit of sleeping with women I like."

The fact that he liked her revved her heart, but it also didn't make sense.

"You only sleep with women you don't like?"

"I only sleep with women who know I'm not the kind of guy to make a commitment."

His voice was so casual, so confident that her spine stiffened. "Are you accusing me of falling in love with you overnight?"

He had the good graces to look sheepish. "No." He paused and combed his fingers through his tousled hair, turning back into her Hugo from the night before. "I'm saying you're special. Nice. A good person. And the last thing I want to do is hurt you."

The admission hadn't been easy for him and her soul melted. The sense that spending more time together might turn him into her Hugo forever raced through her brain, but she stopped it. He was a workaholic who had secrets—

Maybe lots of them.

Plus, his project was at stake. She hadn't been hired to keep him sane, but in a way that's what event planners did. They took care of details so the people who hired them could relax. She'd realized the day before that he had memories that haunted him. She'd been grateful for getting stranded together because it was an opportunity to get to know him well enough to make sure he didn't have a meltdown. Even though he really hadn't told her any secrets—

But maybe he didn't have to? He might not have shared a specific secret, but spending time with him had shown her he had some soft spots. The chink in his armor wasn't *one* thing—one memory about his past—that she had to keep him away from. It was *him*. The nice guy inside him who appeared when he thought of his past.

In a way, that made things easier. She didn't have to probe and ponder, trying to figure out one big secret. All she had to do was make sure he didn't linger too long thinking about his past.

He glanced over. "Want to call room service for breakfast?"

She frowned. "We could have had room service last night?"

He laughed. "Probably not. I'm guessing the kitchen staff that's been experimenting with recipes had already gone for the day. But we could have found something to eat. Still, because you provided dinner, I'd like to repay you with breakfast."

She peered around. She didn't really want the chef and/or waitstaff to come up to the penthouse and find her with Hugo. More than that, though, she'd figured out what she had to do to protect his project. There was no point hanging out too long, getting attached, hoping for something that wouldn't happen.

Saddened by that, but realizing the truth of it, she turned toward the shower again. "I've got a lot of work to do."

He smiled. "Okay." But he rose from the bed. Before she reached the bathroom door, he did. Gloriously naked, he made her heart pitter-patter and some of the better parts of their night together played in her head. Then he caught her upper arms and kissed her gently, and everything inside her told her to forget about work. They only needed more time together for sweet Hugo to come out of hiding and stay out—

But a picture of life with him, another man with secrets, popped into her head, along with the feelings of inadequacy because Josh hadn't confided in her. It might be years before Hugo got comfortable enough that he'd let all of his guard down.

She remembered all the lonely days of living with a guy who had a secret and the horrible pain when she'd realized he *had* confided in someone else.

No.

She didn't want that. Not any of it.

When she finally was ready to date, she'd be looking for someone who treated her like an equal. Someone who trusted her. Someone she could trust.

Sexy—gorgeous—as Hugo Harrington was, he was not the guy for her, and thinking she could change him was foolish.

She eased away and entered the bathroom, ending their one-night stand.

When the penthouse elevator dinged to take Erin downstairs, Hugo headed to the shower.

That had gone well. Not only had he and Erin enjoyed the evening, but her departure made him believe she was on his wavelength. No pouting. No flirting to extend their time. A nice, clean break.

He frowned. Why did that give him an empty feeling in his chest?

Just as she hadn't fallen in love with him overnight, he hadn't fallen for her.

Had he?

Of course not. He wasn't accusing himself of falling in love, but maybe entering those initial stages of liking someone—

No. He'd liked her before last night. And he knew making love added to those feelings, but he was a smart guy. Not about protecting himself but protecting *her*.

He'd stay in line to protect her.

He stepped into the shower. After a quick

scrubbing, he got out and redressed in the clothes from the day before, but when he picked up his shirt a memory slid through him. The lightness of joy that had filled him when she hadn't protested him yanking her T-shirt over her head or when he'd reached for the buttons on this very white shirt.

The memory shivered through him and he shook his head. He had to stop that. He wasn't the kind of guy to dwell on a one-night stand. Especially not one that had gone exactly as it should have. They'd enjoyed each other. But they both knew this shouldn't go any further.

The empty feeling filled his chest again.

Confused, he stopped those crazy thoughts, called the kitchen to order breakfast, texted Ronnie telling him he wouldn't be leaving for the Manhattan team office for another hour, then scrolled through the news on his phone. An hour and a half later, he was with his New York staff, working.

But he couldn't get past the never-before-experienced regret that he really could only have that one night with Erin. His brain edged toward trying to come up with ways or reasons they could spend another night together, and when he realized he was thinking about her again, he stopped it.

Because it was wrong. She was a mum. She

had responsibilities. And he was a lone wolf. His own brother and sister were wary of him because he had left them. Even his mother had let him go. Proving some people weren't made to be loved. Some people were born to be successful, so strong they were off-putting.

Not in a horrible, villainous way. But simply in a way that didn't give them enough time for relationships, enough mental energy.

And Erin absolutely deserved someone who would love her completely.

The thought dinged his heart again, but he ignored it. He was not the guy she needed.

CHAPTER FOUR

ERIN WORKED HARD all morning, happy when her mom brought Noah to her office a little after noon with lunch and a change of clothes.

"Thanks. Not only do I need to get into something clean, but I was starving!"

"No breakfast, I'm guessing," her mom said as she handed Erin her lunch bag full of goodies.

Erin's face reddened. "No. Got right to work."

Her mom glanced around. "Where'd you sleep?"

"There are some finished rooms on the top floor. Hugo took one. I took the other." She blanched internally at the fact that she hadn't mentioned they were part of a penthouse suite. But, really, her no-lying rule was getting ridiculous. Surely there had to be a middle ground.

"I showered, but putting the same clothes back on was icky."

Marge laughed. "You should be glad you

had a shower. Not everybody is so lucky to be stranded in a hotel."

"Right." She bit into her sandwich and groaned with pleasure. "So good."

"You really are starving."

"Yes. I'm guessing the roads are clear if the buses are running."

"London road crews might have needed a little time, but they got the job done."

"Or the snow on the streets melted," Hugo said, entering the office.

His beautiful gray eyes met Erin's and damned if she didn't blush again.

"London weather is odd." He faced Marge. "I see you brought lunch for Erin."

Her mom all but swooned. She'd probably be thrilled if Erin told her they'd spent the night together. "Yes. And lucky thing too since she was starving."

"She shouldn't be. The kitchen is filled with chefs and helpers trying out recipes for the grand opening. They could probably feed her for a week."

He turned to Erin. "When you're through, I'd like to see you in my office."

She nodded and he left.

Marge watched him go. "Have you at least *tried* flirting with him?"

Erin squeezed her eyes shut. She wasn't embarrassed that she'd slept with Hugo. But most grown women didn't tell their mom about their lovers.

"Mom! Seriously! The guy is devoted to work. Even if I fell madly in love with him, he's not the kind to settle down."

"Yeah but think of the fun you could have— and practice for when you are ready for a relationship."

Why did having a no-strings-attached affair suddenly sound like the perfect plan?

Erin shook her head to clear it of the ridiculous thought. She had to get herself back on neutral ground with him so she could watch for those memories that hit him the hardest and steer him away from them.

Plus, no matter what the situation, she would not discuss her sex life with her mother. "Please stop."

Noah toddled up to her and she pulled him onto her lap. They talked about snow and the story his grandmother had read to him the night before. Then Erin told them she really had to get back to work. But she'd be home that night at the regular time.

When they were gone, she raced to a restroom to change into her clean clothes, sighing with relief when she finally felt normal.

But her "normal" quickly disappeared when

she reached Hugo's office and hesitated by the door. She really could have some fun times with him—

No. She knew herself. She wasn't the kind of woman who became someone's lover. She'd always been a romantic looking for true love. Even more now that Josh's betrayals had almost pushed her to believe love didn't exist. It did. It had to. She had friends who had found it. And now that she was actually letting herself think about this, she wanted what they had. Though an affair sounded appealing and logical, eventually she'd fall in love and he wouldn't.

Then she'd be hurt…and he wouldn't.

Her resolve in place, she knocked on his door.

"Come in, Erin."

"Just wanted to make sure I wasn't interrupting."

"I told you to come to my office. That's the definition of not interrupting."

She took the few steps to the chair in front of his desk, looking at his glossy hair, his broad shoulders, and suppressed a sigh. Fantasy Hugo had definitely disappeared some time during the night and Real Hugo was back.

But that was good. They needed to return to the place where he saw her as he had the day before. Someone he employed, but also someone he could trust. Someone he could talk to.

She sat on the chair and opened her notebook. He got right to the ideas he'd come up with the night before.

The night before?

Seriously?

While she was sleeping, sated and happy, nestled against him, he'd gotten out his phone and made notes?

Maybe she'd inspired him?

Maybe she was his muse?

It was such a romantic notion. Being his muse, she'd be like the other half of him. Yin to his yang—

"Erin? Did you get that?"

She snapped to attention, embarrassed to have been caught daydreaming about something she'd already dismissed. "I'm sorry. I got the part about oranges but didn't hear the other thing."

The tips of his ears turned red.

Let him ignore the reason for her lapse in concentration and get them back to work. Please do not let him ask what had her distracted.

"I said my brother remembered the name of the shop where our mum bought stockings that were stuffed for all the kids in attendance."

She sat up. "You talked to your brother?"

"Briefly."

Forgetting all about being his muse, she looked for signs of distress. Anger. Sadness. Anything that might throw him off his game. "This morning?"

His eyes met hers. "Yes."

Her soul forgot to breathe. Those eyes were so rich with emotion and whether it was a good idea, she and Hugo had connected the day before. First getting cocoa, then sleeping together. She knew the significance of him speaking with someone from his family. Family he was having trouble getting along with—

Was that his big worry? Not that a sad memory would spoil his Christmas Eve celebration, but that his family might?

She sucked in a deep draft of air. He might not out and out admit it. But she saw it now. So clearly it amazed her that it took her so long.

He'd mentioned hanging ornaments with his brother and sister. Even asked if she thought they'd come to the Christmas Eve celebration—

"Oh, my gosh. You're worried your brother and sister won't show up."

Hugo gaped at her. She looked cute and huggable in her jeans and sweatshirt and his heart had done a somersault when she'd entered his office, but her words sucked all the air out of his lungs.

"Do you think I shouldn't be?"

"I don't know." She caught his gaze. "It could be a real embarrassment if you have Ornament Hanging Ceremony in the program for your Christmas Eve event but your brother and sister don't attend."

He tapped his pencil on the desk. It was a problem he knew existed but not something he let himself think about too much because he *hoped* they'd see his dedication to the hotel and show up.

Yet she'd homed in on it.

"You know, you could just hang an ornament yourself."

He frowned. "And leave the other two sitting on the table? For everybody to see? An obvious reminder that my brother and sister didn't come?"

"If they decide not to attend, you can gloss right over it by making a big deal out of choosing one of the three ornaments as if it's a last-minute decision, part of the ceremony. Not that all three ornaments need to be hung. Then once you walk away, I'll swoop in and scoop up the other two and whisk them away."

He took a breath, thinking that through. It was perfect and it solved one of his worst worries.

Some of the tightness in his spine loosened. "Okay. That'll work."

"Now, back to the stockings. I can call your brother for the store's name, but I'm going to need at least an estimate of how many I'll need."

Weirdness settled over him. She'd relieved one of his biggest fears and moved on to the next item on her to-do list as if nothing had happened?

He cleared his throat. "You'll need to check with the reservations crew to get the number of kids who will be attending, and that will give you an accurate count for the stockings."

She scribbled some notes. "I might also poke around upstairs a bit, dig around for either an actual stocking or pictures of the stockings."

She looked up and caught his gaze. A bubble of something formed in his chest. She was a pro. So good at what she did, she didn't even realize how fast and how easily she'd helped him.

Joy skipped along his skin, sensitizing it. And he suddenly knew why he kept thinking about her, about their one-night stand. Their time together had been perfect. Spontaneous. Open. Immensely enjoyable.

His aggressive self, the one that always went after what he wanted, wanted her. Again. And maybe again and again.

Maybe every night she was here, in London.

Erin said, "I'm thinking we should get ten or

twelve extra stockings in case there are walk-ins on Christmas Eve."

Hugo's bubble burst. He might want her. But she didn't even appear to be thinking about him. About the possibility of another night together.

"There'll be no walk-ins. We hope to have the place booked."

Her attention fully focused on the notepad she held, she said, "Okay. I'll check with reservations today and every day until the actual event."

He said, "Good thinking," but his pride was a little bruised. While he fought a hellish battle to get himself to stop dwelling on her, she had no problem talking about stockings?

Which was exactly what needed to be happening for the grand opening. The biggest project of his life. The goal he'd been working toward since his stepfather kicked him out.

Plus, she obviously didn't feel the same way he did. He could see himself longing to be with her, if she showed even one sign that she wanted to be with him. But she was a pro. And he was behaving like a smitten fool.

Annoyed with himself, he said, "I'm also toying with the idea of taking the celebration out to the courtyard garden."

Her eyes widened with excitement. "Wow."

"My parents' celebration was wonderful.

Warm and cozy. Though I definitely want those elements in our party... I also want a fresh spin. Does taking it to the garden seem like it would be a fresh spin or sound like too much?"

"What if you have the dinner exactly as it used to be in the ballroom, then have everyone go outside for the visit from Santa?"

He loved her idea but couldn't believe he'd asked for her opinion. He never needed anyone's opinion. If he had an idea, he either used it or he chucked it. Fighting his desire to sleep with her again had knocked him off his game.

Which was another reason to get himself beyond this. To stop wanting something he couldn't have.

He waved his hand, dismissing her. "Anyway, that's it for now."

She smiled and rose from her seat, closing her spiral notebook. He glanced at it, wondering why she didn't take notes on her phone, then realized she had an actual, physical record of everything they discussed, the theme of the event and the work she had done. If something happened to her, her staff probably knew to find that book.

She wasn't merely beautiful and sexy; she was smart. And today he was finding her intelligence every bit as sexy and her shiny red hair—

"I can go?"

"Yes! Yes!" He bounced from his seat and hit his knee on the top of the desk. Damn his wandering thoughts. He was behaving like an idiot.

This stopped now. No more rambling. No more noticing things about her.

They'd had a one-night stand. They worked together. He *employed* her. His mind should have already moved on to other things.

She turned and walked out without so much as a goodbye or a smile and his pride dinged again.

This time he did groan as he lowered himself to his seat. He decided his weird reaction was a result of the pressure of the project and didn't think about it for the rest of the day.

But when it came time to leave the hotel that evening, his thoughts jumped back to her. It wasn't right for her to ride a bus after a twelve-hour day. He couldn't break his promise to make her stay comfortable just because he needed time away from her.

When Erin left the hotel that night, Hugo leaned against his limo door. He looked like a teenage boy waiting for the girl from math class to come out so he could talk to her. The urge to tease him rose in her, along with a yearning to simply be with him.

But she said nothing. They'd had a night of

fun. Neither intended for it to go any further than it had. She needed to keep the objectivity going that she'd cultivated that day—no matter how difficult it was to get their night together out of her head.

"Are you taking me home?"

He opened the door. "Yes. I promised you a nice stay in London. I'm not marring that with late-night bus trips."

"Okay." She slid into the limo.

He got in beside her and reached out to close the glass that separated the passengers from the driver. She frowned. Why would he care if his driver heard their conversation?

She wondered if she'd done something wrong. Except, she hadn't. She made sure every bit of work she did for him was as good as it could be. Her actions always spoke louder than her words. She hadn't done anything wrong.

So what wouldn't he want his driver to hear?

They made the two turns that would take them to her apartment and the limo stayed silent.

Silent. He didn't even say, *How was your day? Any problems with the project? Anything you want to discuss?*

The car stayed quiet.

So she said, "How was your day?"

He glanced over at her with a frown. "What?"

She sighed. "Just making conversation."

"Oh. Okay, then. My day was fine." He smiled briefly, a weird, fake smile. "How was your day?"

"Um…good. I guess. Getting a lot of things done."

"Good."

She took a breath. "And I'm glad your day was fine too."

"Yes. I was too."

The conversation died, but that was better than enduring the stilted discussion of how their days had gone.

She suddenly missed romantic Hugo. That guy knew exactly what to say. But maybe this was for the best? This stilted, emotionless guy was the real Hugo, and no matter how much she yearned for things to be different, *this* was reality.

She tried to shove that truth into her brain so hard it stuck, but memories of him being sweet and kind, sexy and romantic kept writing over them.

It was going to be harder than she thought to forget about their one-night stand.

CHAPTER FIVE

THE NEXT MORNING, Erin immediately went to the attic to search for stockings. Stooped in front of a big box, she might have stopped at the first sample she'd found, but it wasn't alone. Two different stockings had been stored together.

She rocked back on her heels. She should ask Hugo if the hotel purchased one kind of stocking for boys and one for girls. Or one for older kids and one for younger kids. Or a different kind of stocking every year, making each year's offering a keepsake.

But, frankly, she wasn't in the mood to see him.

She told herself that wasn't good. The guy was her biggest client. It shouldn't matter one way or another if they hadn't been able to have a decent conversation in his limo the night before. Or that the horrible attempt at chitchat had actually made her long for romantic Hugo.

She squeezed her eyes shut. *It doesn't matter.*

Except she was back to thinking about him again, wishing things could be different when she knew they couldn't.

And she had a job to do.

She snatched the two stockings from the floor as she rose and headed to the attic door.

She would set their relationship right simply by going to his office and asking about the stockings. She would be the nicest person on the planet to him. She would not fail. *He* would not fail.

Because, damn it, that's what she did! Made everything perfect for her clients.

She stormed to the general manager's space Hugo used when he was in the hotel, but he hadn't arrived yet. His habit was to come in around ten or so and stay a few hours, but that schedule wasn't etched in stone. If he needed time with the staff in charge of the renovations, he'd stay with the team of New York employees as long as he needed. If he needed to come back to the hotel in the afternoon, he did that. He floated around, being where he had to be to get things done. And he wasn't here now. Apparently, he didn't need to be.

She turned to leave as the office phone rang.

Pivoting to face the desk again, she stared at it. She hadn't realized the landlines had been hooked up. Everybody was using their cell, if only for convenience. Running back and forth between the hotel and office, Hugo was easier to reach that way. And she could be reached anywhere in the hotel, or at the florists, the bakery or any one of her vendors.

The phone rang again.

She inched into the room. It seemed rude not to answer it. Especially since it could be Hugo calling…

No. He'd call her cell. He wouldn't even know she was in this room.

It rang again.

Damn it! She wasn't the kind of person who didn't answer a ringing phone.

She raced to the desk, catching the receiver as the phone rang one more time. "Hello?"

"Who is this?" a female voice asked. "Isn't this the Harrington Park Hotel?"

"Yes. I'm sorry. I'm not a receptionist. I just happened to be in the office waiting for…someone when you called."

"Would that someone be my brother Hugo?"

Erin's breath caught. *Hugo's sister?*

"Yes. He's usually at the hotel by now, but he must have gotten tied up with his regular staff at the office."

"Aren't you in an office?"

She winced. "I'm in an office at the hotel. I'm

Erin Hunter, the event planner organizing the Christmas Eve celebration."

"Ah, you're the miracle worker he hired."

Erin frowned at the phone. "I wouldn't know about miracle worker, but I do like to get things done."

"Don't mind my mood. I'm Sally, by the way. I'm not usually this grumpy but things are progressing weirdly on the garden."

Intrigued, Erin sat. "Anything I can do to help?"

"No. But I need to talk to my brother. Can you have him ring me?"

"Sure." She frowned again. "Why not just call his cell?"

Sally cleared her throat. "He gave me the number, but I threw it away."

Erin's heart broke a little. She knew how much Hugo wanted his sister at the ornament ceremony and she'd tossed away his number. Still, having Hugo call Sally might be a good first step to settling their differences.

"Okay. Sure. I'll have him call you." She paused, then said, "Does he have *your* number?"

"Yes. My cell." She laughed. "Unless he tossed it."

Erin waited a second as Sally rattled off her number. "Thanks... Um... I could give you his number if you'd like."

Sally paused a little too long. Giving Erin the sense she didn't want any part of Hugo in her life.

Finally, she said, "You know what? I'm just going to send him an email. And, Erin… Don't let my brother run you off the way he does most other people."

Something about that hit Erin oddly. But the quiet in the limo ride home the night before suddenly made sense. Had he been trying to run her off? Not as a subcontractor. He'd made it abundantly clear that he liked her work and wanted her to stay.

Running her off was personal.

"Actually, we've worked together for years."

"So that must be the secret to getting along with him. Have something he wants."

Erin almost said, "Maybe." But decided against it. Hugo was her boss and she wouldn't badmouth him to his family. In fact, everything about the conversation seemed wrong. Hugo should have been the one talking to Sally, not her.

She said, "I'll give him your number."

"No. No. I'll email him."

Erin said, "Okay. Fine." Then she and Sally said their goodbyes.

Though she had tons of work to do, her mind spun with possibilities of what Sally might want.

She was still in Hugo's seat when he walked into the office.

"Problem?"

Caught, she bounced to attention. "No… Yes. Maybe. I—" She stopped her babbling. "Two things. I have a question and your sister, Sally, called."

She handed him the slip of paper with Sally's number and his lips lifted into a smile as he glanced down to read it. But when he saw only Sally's number, he frowned and looked up at Erin again.

"She has my number." His frown grew. "Yet she called on the landline?"

"Yes." The troubled expression on his face wouldn't let her tell him that Sally had tossed his cell number.

"We didn't really chat." Damn it. She suddenly found herself in choppy waters again. Holding back information. Downplaying the call. When she'd sworn to herself that she'd always be honest. Painfully honest.

She took a breath. "Your sister was confused because I'd answered the phone that she'd thought you'd answer. That's all."

That and Sally had clearly let Erin know she wasn't Hugo's biggest fan.

Damn it. No matter how honest she wanted to be, she couldn't say that. Wasn't there some sort of etiquette about this? Like: if you can't say something nice, don't say anything at all?

Yes! That was it! Her mom had said that all the time when Erin was a little girl.

Plus, if she really wanted to get bottom-line honest on this… Getting Sally to the Christmas Eve celebration might fall under Erin's purview, but Hugo's relationship with his sister was none of her business. She had no responsibility to tell Hugo her conclusions and suspicions.

It wasn't like holding back a cancer diagnosis.

She took another breath as her thoughts simultaneously cleared about Sally and muddled about Josh. The pain of his holding that back rolled through her once again. No matter how hard she tried, or how many other circumstances she compared it to, his not telling her had been unforgiveable.

"Anyway, she said she'd email you to discuss the garden. And I wanted to talk about the Christmas stockings."

He rounded the desk as she scooted to the front. "What about the stockings?"

"I found two styles of stockings in a box. If they had been in two different boxes, I might have assumed your parents bought a unique stocking for every year…sort of like a keepsake. But they were in the same box, making me wonder if younger kids and older kids got different stockings or boys and girls?"

"Different stockings every year. All kids get the same one."

"So, they are like a keepsake?"

He dropped to his seat. "I guess. I never saved mine…"

"Maybe your mother did?"

His frown deepened as he glanced at some papers on his desk, as if his attention was off the stockings and moving on because he had too much work to do to dawdle.

"I think those are requisitions dropped off by subcontractors."

"I know what they are."

His tone caused her to step back, as she reminded herself that he was working to create emotional distance between them—

Except he was also a guy whose sister had tossed his cell number.

She remembered the happily surprised expression on his face when he'd been told his sister had called and how it had shifted when he saw she'd only left a number for him to return her call. What if that had really hurt him? Erin knew he wanted his sister and brother at the Christmas Eve celebration.

He was renovating the family hotel.

He'd given his siblings a role in the new hotel.

*What if he wanted to reunite? What if he'd
spent millions of dollars buying this run-down
building and millions more renovating it? Not
just to recreate his past, but to reunite his
family?*

The truth of it hit so hard, she almost had to
sit.

"Erin?"

"What?" She shook her head to bring herself back to the present. "I'm sorry. What were
you saying?"

She glanced at his face and saw lines she'd
missed before this. She saw sadness in his gray
eyes. Not the emptiness of not caring as she'd
always believed. But a bone-deep sadness.

"I said we get new stockings every year.
Go crazy picking out a new design or find the
stockings from the first year and buy those."
He frowned. "Though I'm not sure how you'd
know which stocking had been chosen for the
first year my parents had this celebration."

"Boxes aren't marked."

He dismissed her by looking down at his
work again. "Figure it out. It doesn't matter either way. A new stocking type or find the first
one."

She backed up, inching toward the open door.
"Okay."

"Close that."

She nodded, but as she closed the door her heart hurt, and guilt tiptoed through her for being so angry with him for making things difficult in the limo the night before.

A man who'd been estranged from his family for so long might not know how to make a connection.

Of course, he was the one who'd left his family. So, wasn't it true that he had no one to blame but himself?

Thursday afternoon concluded with a short meeting with the subcontractors doing the renovation work. Hugo strode into the conference room, his jacket off, his tie loose and his sleeves rolled up. This was the real work. Jay had the kitchen and menu under control. Sally had some problems with the courtyard garden, but he had every confidence in her. His brother and sister had become remarkable adults.

And Erin would make the celebration perfect.

Even as he thought the last, he saw her sitting on one of the chairs around the conference table, laughing with the construction supervisor.

Annoyance skittered through him at the sight of her so easygoing and happy with another man, along with that silly joy he always felt when she was around. The joy he had to fight so hard to ignore he could only talk about work with her. Which made riding home in the limo quiet and awkward.

"Good afternoon, everyone."

The men and women at the conference table came to attention at the sound of his voice.

"I hope everyone's got a good report for me."

General murmurs of agreement floated around him as he sat.

"Except for Ms. Hunter, whose presence confuses me."

"I need reports too," Erin said, totally unaffected by his negativism. "I need to know when rooms will be done so I can assign decorating crews." She caught his gaze. Her blue eyes held an emotion that confused him. She should be on her high horse, her pride radiating like the rays of the sun because he'd questioned her presence. Instead, she studied him as if he were a bug under a microscope.

"Plus, I want to check their pics from other Christmas Eve celebrations to see if I can piece together which photos are from the first party... and if any one of them shows the Christmas stockings."

His breath stuttered. He'd told her it didn't matter if she figured out which of the stockings were from the first celebration, but it did. He wanted to do this right and, as always, she understood that and was trying to make it happen.

She smiled slightly, knowing she'd pleased him.

His heart warmed and that silly joy filled him to overflowing. He cleared his throat, but the warmth stayed with him. His voice was gruff when he said, "Everybody hand over their pictures. Let Erin examine them."

"I'll get them back to you," she promised with a smile, as the supervisors who had the pictures pulled them from clipboards or file folders and passed them down the table.

Hugo's head tilted. He'd seen charming people finagle their own way all the time. He'd seen bossy people force their way on others. But he'd never seen anyone softly, sweetly lure everyone in the way Erin did.

She smiled at him and gave him a quick nod as if to say he could go on to the first item on his list, and for a few seconds he only stared at her.

Everything about her was so damned easy. Even making love had been so natural and simple that maybe he'd missed part of the beauty of it.

With a shake of his head, he told himself he was crazy or going soft and that could not happen. He had a job to do. He asked a question of the general contractor who began to give his report, but Hugo's gaze strayed to Erin again.

He'd been rude to her the night before. Snippy with her that morning. Yet here she was, her normal self.

No. She'd realized the Christmas stockings from the first celebration had meaning for him and she was going out of her way to find them.

People were always trying to please him. Employees. Subcontractors. Vendors. But this was personal. He could feel it.

He knew it when she sent him a soft smile when she noticed him staring at her.

His heart flipped in his chest. A million confusing thoughts assaulted him. But the one that stuck was that he'd like to be back in bed with her. His head on a pillow, his arm around her shoulders tucking her beside him.

Crazy.

Seriously. He was protecting *her*. Why couldn't he get a handle on this?

"And that's where we stand, big picture–wise."

Arnie Simmons leaned back in his chair, ending his report, and Hugo leaned back too. He'd missed every damned word the man had said because he'd been fixating on Erin.

The painting supervisor went up next and Hugo paid attention as if his life depended on it. The truth was, he'd sleep with Erin again in a New York minute. Hell, he'd sleep with her every day until the project was over and maybe once or twice in Manhattan after they returned.

But he wouldn't ever settle down and that would hurt her.

And in that moment, he made a vow never, ever to hurt her. In every possible way, she was too good for him.

Sadness replaced the longing that had filled him, but he accepted the pain of it. He knew who he was. Knew there were a lot of things he'd never have because he didn't make those kinds of commitments.

CHAPTER SIX

FRIDAY MORNING, HUGO strode into the Harrington Park Hotel feeling better. Scaffolding had been moved from the lobby to the ballroom where painting had begun. Yet another step was complete. Things were proceeding on schedule. Not a ripple of change had been made in the original plan, and that bolstered his belief that they really were going to do this. They would have the hotel up and running and the most amazing Christmas Eve celebration.

And nothing anyone said or did that day could ruin his mood.

Then he saw Erin bounding down the hall toward him, her movements easy and fluid in her blue jeans and simple gray T-shirt.

Her smile was quick and genuine. "Can I have five minutes?"

He forced a smile so she wouldn't notice his heart burst with that damned joy again. He'd had this conversation with himself yesterday.

His inability to get ahold of himself was an aberration. Once he set his mind to something, he did it.

"Sure. Follow me into the office." He walked in, tossed his briefcase on the desk and took off his overcoat.

"I have a delivery scheduled for tomorrow."

"So?" He knew the next day was Saturday, but *she* knew working Saturdays was always on the table with a deadline this close.

"I promised Noah I'd take him sightseeing tomorrow. If I can't, I'm not sure how I'll make it up to him. So I thought I'd simply switch days. There's not a lot on today's agenda for me. I'd like to take today to show him the sights and work tomorrow."

It made perfect sense. And if he hadn't been distracted by the way her hair seemed to pick up light and make it shimmer, he might have immediately said yes. Now he had to fake annoyance.

"There are always things you can do here."

"Or I could take my son to see the sights on a day that's light with work, as you promised I could."

Thank goodness he'd made the promise. He looked down at his work. He gruffly said, "Okay, fine." But he felt a little guilty for kind of punishing her for something that was his problem. He was the one having trouble being around her. She was fine. It was time to act accordingly.

He glanced up at her. "You know what? You're right. Today's a perfect day to take him sightseeing."

Her face filled with surprise. "Really?"

"Yeah. I'm always semiprepared for bad news. That's why I reacted poorly. Don't mind me."

And that was as close as he would get to either an apology or an explanation. He did have a reputation for being a grouch to protect.

But he also realized that it wasn't her fault that he was so drawn to her. Plus, he was the one who had seduced her, and look at how easily she'd adapted to it meaning nothing even though what they'd shared had been *something*.

It really had.

She said, "Thanks. I'll see you tomorrow."

"And, Erin, don't forget to take Noah to Southbank."

"That's the first place we're going."

"Good. We'll talk tomorrow."

She walked out of his office. Knowing she couldn't see, he watched the sway of her hips, remembering the way they'd felt beneath his hands.

Everything about her and that night had been perfect. If he were a sappier kind of guy, he might have mooned over her.

Wait—

Wasn't that what he was doing? Noticing light dancing in her hair. Jealous when one of his supervisors had made her laugh. Watching her graceful walk.

Identifying the problem put everything into perspective and he settled in to work. Telling himself that now that he'd figured things out, he'd be better. He especially hoped she had a great time with Noah and that Noah enjoyed the sights.

He frowned, wondering if she'd know where to take her son other than Southbank. After all, she spent twelve to fourteen hours a day in *this hotel*. She hadn't seen any sights herself. Probably didn't know anything about London—

He remembered how she'd loved Southbank. What a great day that had been. How nice it had felt to be outside. How nice it had been to think about Christmas, see it blossoming all around them, without relating it back to the hotel.

He'd spent the last decades thinking of nothing but acquiring the family hotel and reuniting with his brother and sister, and it was working. Sally might be standoffish, but he swore he'd win her over. But suddenly today, he wondered how much of life he'd missed. What had passed him by because he'd been consumed by this hotel?

His skin began to itch. The room felt small and tight.

He thought of Erin again. If he closed his eyes and let himself go, he could feel her smooth skin against his. He could remember her laugh. He also recalled his promise to her that she'd show her son a different view of Christmas and though she could do that all by herself, the strange sense that he owed her overwhelmed him. Not only had he promised, but also he'd been grumpy with her when he was the one who couldn't get *her* out of his mind.

That had been so wrong.

He sprang out of his seat. He couldn't let her go on thinking he was a grinch. And he knew how to fix it. His workload was broader and more encompassing than Erin's, but he could afford a day off too.

He had his driver take him to Southbank, knowing he might be early or that he might not even find her in the crowd. Then his cell phone buzzed with a text from a subcontractor and he smiled. He could find her. All he had to do was call her and ask where she was.

Erin stared at the phone after finishing her call with Hugo.

He *wanted* to make sure she and Noah saw all the right things?

More unexpected, he was taking the day off… for *her*?

She pushed Noah's stroller in the direction of Jubilee Park, where they'd arranged to meet.

When he walked up to her, still in his suit for work and cashmere overcoat, her heart skipped a beat. He might only be playing the role of kind boss, or honest negotiator who intended to keep his promise, but when she looked at him, her thoughts drifted back to their night together.

When he'd laughed.

When he'd kissed her with abandon and loved her like a man starved for intimacy.

And maybe he was. Watching him so closely these past few days, she'd noticed things he couldn't hide and drawn conclusions about his longing to recreate his past. Then, having spoken with Sally, she understood his fears. While he labored to bring his family together, there was no guarantee that his family wanted *him* in their lives.

She almost couldn't comprehend that. Her father had divorced her mom when Erin was too young to remember, leaving her without an extended family because her dad remarried and moved on. Plus, her mom had been the only child of a couple who had emigrated from Ireland. They'd been alone until Josh. Erin had thought she'd begun building the family she and her mom had yearned for. Then Josh had died.

She'd always believed people with siblings were lucky because siblings were close, there for each other.

But something had happened to ruin the Harringtons. Not just their hotel. And whether Hugo was the perpetrator of the disaster or the victim wasn't as cut-and-dried as she'd originally thought.

Unless he was sorry that he'd broken up his family? And not trying to recreate an idyllic past but trying to make amends?

"Hey."

She smiled at him. Evil villain or misunderstood, tormented soul, she didn't know. But she *was* happy to have someone who knew London to show her and her son around.

And maybe—just maybe—he'd explain some of his life.

"Hey."

He stooped to Noah's level. "And how are you today?"

Noah glanced down and mumbled, "Good."

Erin said, "He'll be happy once we start moving."

Hugo rose. "I get that. He's a man of action."

For some reason that made Noah giggle. Hugo's face transformed. He glanced down at the little boy as if he were an absolute miracle and Erin's heart stuttered. She suddenly saw not a successful guy or an exacting, grouchy boss, but a guy who'd lived his entire adult life without a connection to anyone.

He pointed to the building behind them. "There's a sea-life aquarium in there. I think he'll love it."

Erin pushed the stroller toward the building with Hugo lifting the front end to make short work of the steps. He paid their admission and Erin decided not to argue. While things were good between them, she had the perfect opportunity to observe. Or maybe just enjoy his company.

But only two minutes into the aquarium, Noah began to fuss. Hugo glanced down at him and Erin held her breath. He looked away from Noah, around the space, and said, "In that stroller, he's two feet below everything." He reached down and loosened the straps. "Hey, bud. Do you want to walk, or do you want me to carry you?"

Amazed, Erin said, "It might do him good to walk around a bit."

When they had Noah on his feet, Hugo frowned. "But he's still too short to see."

"How about if we let him walk until we reach

an exhibit. Then we can take turns lifting him to see."

Hugo nodded. "Sounds like a plan."

The time in the aquarium passed quickly. They'd started off taking turns holding Noah and showing him the sea life, but soon Hugo simply kept him. The little boy and happy man bonded right before her eyes, making her heart ache. Noah needed a male influence as much as Hugo needed a family. And if he were anybody else, she'd believe this was fate. But she couldn't forget he might be the villain in his family drama.

They took Noah outside to a vendor for lunch, which they ate at a table under a tent. But after that, Noah began to fuss again. Erin didn't blame him. She might like the shops and opportunity to look for gifts for her mom, but her son was obviously bored.

"I guess neither one of us thought about how interested a three-year-old would be sitting in a stroller while I browsed through shops."

Hugo laughed. "Actually, I have the perfect place to take him. Trust me?"

Seeing him so happy, she smiled. "Sure."

After calling Hugo's driver, they put the stroller into the trunk of the limo and headed off. When the car stopped in front of Hamleys toy store, Erin gasped. "It's adorable!"

The red facade and red awnings were dressed for the holiday. As she stepped out of the limo, waiting for Ronnie to bring Noah's stroller, she paused and breathed in the cold December air. All this time she'd been worried about Hugo, but she suddenly realized how much she'd needed a break too.

Hugo and Ronnie took over the job of getting Noah into his stroller, and then Hugo pushed him to the store, Erin on his heels.

Joy warmed her. She forgot all about Hugo's troubles because he had. Noah laughed and looked from side to side, amazed by all the toys and people.

They followed the crowd, slowing down to let Noah examine a toy or laugh at the magician. When they reached a set of stairs, Hugo lifted Noah out of his stroller, then texted Ronnie to come in and get the stroller and stow it in the limo.

"He needs to be up high to see all this," Hugo said as they climbed the steps.

Noah seemed to be in awe. The toys and Christmas carols had lulled him into a state of blissful shock. They spent a few minutes in a room with elves who helped him write his Christmas list for Santa, and then they took the short walk into the room where the man himself sat on a throne.

"Come on back, young man."

Hugo slid Noah to the floor and urged him to go see Santa. He shyly stepped forward until he reached the man with the red suit and white beard.

Erin said, "You can sit on his lap."

But Noah didn't look predisposed to doing that and took two steps back.

Santa laughed. "Oh, that's okay." He winked. "If you just want to tell me your list I'll remember."

Still dumbstruck, Noah handed Santa the list he'd created with the elves and when Santa took it, he raced back to his mom.

Hugo laughed. "I like his style. He gets right to the point. His list has what he wants. No need for technicalities like sitting on his lap."

Erin scooped him up. "Did you like Santa?"

The little boy grinned.

They waved goodbye and Santa said, "Ho! Ho! Ho!"

Noah beamed, clearly pleased with the experience.

As they turned to leave, Hugo said, "Did you happen to take note of what was on that list?"

"Memorized it."

"Good. I had something in mind to get him, but if you'd rather I buy him one of the toys on the list, I'm okay with that."

Her heart tugged but warning bells went off. He was behaving like a guy dating Noah's mom. That wasn't their deal. Especially since he'd said they'd only have one night and then made a point to distance himself from her. "You don't have to get him a gift."

"Are you kidding? He's the first kid I've had in my life in... I don't know how long. The first chance I've ever had to buy a child's gift. I want it."

Erin peeked at him as they headed toward the stairs and to the limo. It was the most telling thing he'd ever said. Even if he had been the villain in his family drama, he'd obviously suffered for what he'd done.

They piled into the car and Hugo glanced at his watch. "I'm guessing he needs to get home."

"Yes."

He looked over at her. "This was actually a very fun day for me. Thank you."

"Thank you!" Erin said. "I might have eventually figured out to take him to see Santa, but having a limo makes everything easier."

Hugo laughed and her heart tugged again. She'd never seen him this relaxed. And this might be the perfect time to get him to talk.

"I'd be happy to make you dinner to pay you back."

He faced her. His eyes softened, but he shook

his head. "That's okay. I'm going to go to the hotel to see if there were any problems today."

"Yeah." Erin winced. "That might be a good idea."

"Besides, your mum probably missed you two and she'll want some time."

Erin rolled her eyes. "A few days ago, my mom realized how close we were to Ireland and she became obsessed with finding her relatives."

"She has relatives in Ireland?"

"Her parents moved to the US when they got married. Mom was born in the United States and her parents eventually became citizens, but both sides of her extended family are in Ireland."

"Oh."

"When she and my dad divorced, she stayed in the United States to give me a chance to get to know my dad. But he was never really interested. When he remarried and started another family, he totally dropped me, and my mom and I sort of became a team. But now that I'm working and have Noah, some days I think she feels alone… She wants to know where she came from. Who her people are."

Hugo's face saddened. "I get that."

Erin could have kicked herself. Of course, he understood that! He'd lost his family too.

"Anyway," she said, trying to get the conversation away from things that clearly upset him. "She'll probably jibber jabber all night about what she discovered today. Best for you to get away before she bores you to tears."

He chuckled. "I think it's great."

Warmth filled her. This was the real Hugo. The normal Hugo. The guy he was when he wasn't everybody's boss. The guy she liked. The guy she suspected he wanted to be...but couldn't.

But why couldn't he be? What stopped him?

The limo pulled up to her building, and she and Noah got out as Hugo and Ronnie retrieved the stroller.

"Don't open it. I'll carry him up."

Hugo turned to Ronnie. "And I'll carry the stroller."

They headed into the building, walked into the foyer and turned toward the first apartment on the right.

She opened the door and let Noah run inside, into her mom's arms. Closing the door, she looked up at Hugo and smiled. "Thank you for a lovely day."

"It was my pleasure."

She could see from the light in his eyes that it had been his pleasure. Time spun out between them. The day had been perfect, and they weren't strangers. They'd been lovers. A kiss would be the normal way to end their time together.

But he'd made it clear that their one night was their one night—

He leaned the stroller against the wall by the door, then bent down and touched his lips to hers.

Her lungs froze, but her heart bumped to life. His mouth was familiar, his kiss like coming home. Pure bliss poured through her.

He pulled away. Their gazes clung. Caught in a haze of happiness, she couldn't speak.

Then she realized he was as ecstatic as she was. Her brooding, wounded, confusing boss grinned at her.

"I'll see you tomorrow."

Her smile grew. "Yeah. Tomorrow."

Happiness morphed into something more. A feeling so deep and rich it filled all the empty corners of her soul, as Hugo turned away and headed for the exit.

Dazed, she opened the door and walked into her apartment.

Clearly waiting for her, her mother bounced off the sofa. "Oh, Erin! It's the most wonderful thing! Not only do my parents' relatives remember them…they want to meet me."

Acutely aware of the importance of family acceptance because of Hugo, she said, "That's great."

"They're so kind and so happy that I found them, they're paying for me to go to Ireland. I leave tomorrow!"

Erin blinked. "Tomorrow?"

"Don't worry. They're also making arrangements for Noah. They want to meet him too. And you, when you're not busy with the hotel."

Having trouble keeping up with her mother's news after Hugo's sweet kiss, Erin slid out of her coat. "That's even better."

Her mom studied her face. "What's wrong?"

"Nothing!" She should be confused. But she wasn't. She liked Hugo and he really liked her. She felt like a high school girl after her first real date. A little awed this was happening, but so happy it didn't matter.

"Well, whatever the case, kiss Noah goodbye tomorrow. We'll be gone a few days… But the tickets are open-ended in case my relatives are crazy or we don't get along."

Erin laughed and her mother left the room in a flurry of excitement, wanting to pack.

To keep herself from thinking about how she'd miss Noah, Erin focused on putting her little boy to bed, then the work she needed to do on Saturday, but as soon as she thought of her job, she remembered she'd be seeing Hugo and her heart stopped.

Her mom and son would be gone for four days.

She had no reason not to spend every second of every night with Hugo.

Except, in the end, what if what they felt came to nothing? They'd go their separate ways. And she'd be—

Empty again.

Her heart ached just thinking about it. Josh might have been gone for over three years, but she keenly remembered the pain of losing him. She might lose Hugo for a totally different reason, but a loss was a loss.

Still—

What if what they felt was real?

What if they spent the next few days together and all these crazy emotions floating around in her turned into something real?

Love.

With a guy she would have sworn didn't know what love was.

But maybe being alone for so long had taught him the importance of connection? She'd always believed that if they spent enough time together, he'd tell her his secrets, and after today she was sure of it.

And maybe it would be the biggest mistake of her life not to take this chance?

CHAPTER SEVEN

HUGO SILENTLY RODE in the back of his limo, his thoughts jumbled, the sights and sounds of London passing unnoticed.

When he kissed Erin, his troubles disappeared… Hell, the world disappeared. Totally in the moment, he felt sensations and desires that he never even knew existed.

But as much as he liked her, the emotions, the *needs* scared him. He longed to be with her, to tell her things, to do things—like watch her son's reaction at the hotel's Christmas Eve celebration. But he knew part of that was the intrinsic yearning for a family, a place to belong.

His heart stumbled at the thought. He'd dedicated his life to getting wealthy enough to buy Harrington Park Hotel, to reuniting the family that had rejected him, but what if his real need was to create his own family? Jay spoke to him, worked with him, but there was a reserve, a distance there. And Sally—well, Sally might always hate him.

He didn't really understand his siblings' side of the story. How could he? How could he know what Nick had told them about why he'd left? The man had cleverly framed him for the embezzlement he himself had committed. Nick hadn't done that merely to save his skin. Getting Hugo out of the way would have been the perfect foil. He'd cleared his name and most likely manufactured leverage with the twins. Instead of having them pine for their older brother, Nick had clearly given them reason to hate him.

All those years of sending Christmas cards filled with his hope that someday the family could be together again had fallen on deaf ears and minds set against him. With Sally continuing to keep her distance, he was beginning to wonder if his true path might be to create his own family.

But two things were off about that. First, he loved Jay and Sally. He'd loved being a big brother. The bonds of family shouldn't be so easily snapped. Yet theirs had been.

Second, wasn't he shortchanging Erin to "decide" to create a family, so he chose her—

His limo stopped at his building, and he bade Ronnie good-night and stepped out. Walking inside, he snorted at his thoughts. He wasn't deciding to create a new family, so he chose Erin. Erin made him long for all the things he'd yearned for his entire life. She wasn't by any stretch of the imagination a simple choice. The feelings she inspired were like dynamite, blasting him out of his set ways to consider a kind of life he'd never believed was right for him.

He rode the elevator and stepped into the luxurious penthouse, but that only tripped a whoosh of longing. He had everything—absolutely everything a man could want—except someone to share it with.

And this woman who set his blood on fire, even as she tempted him with a sense of family, a sense of belonging, closeness, intimacy, was the one he wanted to bring here, to spoil, to share with.

Everything got so confused that he reached for his phone the second he shrugged out of his overcoat.

He hit the contact for Jay. The phone rang twice, and then his younger brother answered.

"Hey, Hugo! What's up?"

Slowly lowering himself to his sofa, he said, "Nothing...really."

"Oh, that's a tone of voice I've never heard from you. Something's definitely up. And it's not nothing."

He took a breath. "I don't know. I just feel weird."

Jay laughed. "Weird?"

"Out of sorts."

"Maybe the project is getting to you. You gave us one hell of a deadline. Maybe the pressure is finally over the top?"

"No. Believe it or not, I've handled worse."

"Seriously?"

"Yes." Loosening his tie, Hugo leaned back and settled on the sofa. This was what he needed. A conversation with the twin who was at least willing to give their family a chance. If this didn't get him back to normal, nothing would.

Jay said, "So how are things going at the hotel?"

"Everything's organized chaos. Though it looks like a Greek tragedy, it's actually on schedule."

"How about the party?"

"Erin's on top of it. Even the ridiculous details. And I can be exacting, but that doesn't bother her. She is so attuned to me that even when I assure her that the type of stocking that she chooses for the kids isn't that important, she knows it is and she works to get me what I want."

There was a pause before Jay said, "You like her."

"Of course, I like her. If all my employees were as able to please me as she is, I'd never have a care in the world."

Jay laughed. "No. I mean, I recognize that you like working with her, but you like her as more."

Hugo ran his hand down his face. "Is it that obvious?"

"Maybe not to an outsider, but I think I know you a little better than most people. You had a sense of responsibility when you worked at the hotel back when Mum and Dad owned it, but you always had time for Sally and me."

He had.

He sank a little deeper into the sofa, as his memories of being a big brother flowed through him and he remembered why he was so eager to bring his family back together. Not just for himself, but for his brother and sister too.

"You don't want to have feelings for this woman?"

"I don't think now is the time." He sighed. It should have felt odd talking about things he usually didn't discuss. But he'd once been close to Jay and confiding in his younger brother felt so right, he couldn't stop himself. "There have always been women in my life but not someone I feel these odd things for."

"Maybe it does have something to do with the project?"

He laughed.

"I'm serious. Maybe things seem different because you're under a lot of pressure and you need to let off steam."

"That sounds kind of callous toward the woman."

"No. No. I'm not saying use her. I'm just saying if the two of you like each other why not run with it? Is she having as much fun as you are?"

He remembered their night together, then the trip that afternoon with her son, and he smiled. "Of course."

"Then you're not hurting anybody. And you should let go a little bit."

It might not seem callous, but it did seem risky. He'd never, ever even considered having a serious relationship with a woman and if he tried and failed, he'd hurt her. "I don't think so."

"I do!"

"I don't want to hurt her."

"What if you don't?" Jay sighed. "What if this is the real thing?"

"What if it's not?"

"Did you ever stop to think she's available too because she needs the break as much as you do?"

Feeling his resolve weakening, Hugo closed his eyes. "She probably does. I can be pretty demanding."

Jay laughed. "That's an understatement if I've ever heard one. Look at this like a mutually satisfying agreement. If you ever get the sense that she's uncomfortable, back off. But as long as you're both having fun… For God's sake, have some fun."

"That is how I usually look at things." But those women weren't widows with children.

"Good. Then get back to that. Have some fun. I know how hard you work. You simply need a little bit of downtime."

He chuckled. Talking things out with Jay had made him feel much better. Stronger. In control. He and Jay talked a bit about the hotel, both careful not to mention Sally, who was a touchy subject, and then they said good-night.

Hugo went to bed refusing to think about Erin. Their night together had been amazing. The day with her son had been wonderful. But he was a businessman. The hotel had to come first.

He fell into a deep, rich sleep and woke Saturday morning feeling like a tiger, a man a week away from the biggest success of his life.

His conversation with his brother had more than bolstered him. It had made him realize that he and Jay were growing close again. Even if he didn't turn his family back into the tight unit they'd been before Nick entered the picture, he and Jay would be okay. And he would have his sister in his life somehow—

He shouldn't give up on his plan to make the Harrington family whole again.

After a quick shower and breakfast, he was driven to the office with his New York staff, most of whom were growing eager to go home. He gave a short, inspirational speech, thanked them for helping him complete the project that had always been closest to his heart, urged them to hang in there and sent everyone back to his or her desk ready to do their best work.

Riding the limo to the hotel and walking through the almost complete lobby, he was refreshed. Renewed. His old self. Ready to take on the world.

He sat at his desk and dived into the stack of papers in front of him. Then Erin walked in and a whoosh of desire burned through him, even as his heart did a funny flip.

The temptation was strong to rise and kiss her senseless, which not only confused him, it pushed him back to the place he was before, before he'd spoken with Jay. Filled with a need so intense—something that braided sexual desire, a longing for intimacy and a yearning to create something special with her—he stayed in his seat, dumbfounded.

"Good morning, Hugo."

Her bright, chipper voice warmed his heart, which stuttered to a stop. She was gorgeous even in her jeans and T-shirt. Her kisses were sweet. Making love with her had been amazing…

But her friendship was important to him. And the hotel even more so. He had to get himself back on track.

He cleared his throat. "It's Saturday. Though we took yesterday off, you know it would have been okay to come in late today."

She shrugged. "I have that delivery plus a few other things to do. If I get through them all, I probably won't have to come in tomorrow— Sunday. Sunday's a better day off."

His stuttering heart faltered even more. He used the same principle to get himself to go the extra mile, work harder, get things done.

His voice was thin and gruff when he said, "That's fine. But don't stay all day. I'm sure Noah would like more than a peek at you before bedtime."

She took the seat in front of his desk. For a good thirty seconds she said nothing. Then she raised her gaze to Hugo's and said, "Noah's not home. Neither is my mom." She paused as if letting that information sink in. "You know those Irish relatives I told you she was searching for?"

Confused, he nodded.

"She found them. They got her and Noah tickets to fly to Dublin where a gaggle of them are apparently going to pick her up and take her to their small town."

He blinked. Not just because it seemed sudden that Marge had found her people and wanted time with them, but because he knew why Erin was unexpectedly nervous. She had no responsibilities at home for days. If he wanted, he could be with her every night that her little family was in Ireland.

His brain immediately said, *Yes*. But his throat tightened, and his chest froze. His conversation with Jay played in his head. If they both needed some fun, some stress relief in this final week before the grand opening, they could have days and nights together. Alone. Happy. And no one had to be any the wiser.

Their gazes held a few seconds more as all the possibilities rolled through him, luxurious dinners, passionate nights—

The want of it overwhelmed him and he couldn't stop himself from saying, "So, does this mean we can have dinner at Alain Ducasse?"

Her eyes widened. "Are you kidding?"

He frowned. "I'm not sure if that's a yes or a no."

"I didn't bring the clothes for it."

Her hesitation brought the tiger back—the

guy who didn't let anything get in the way of what he wanted. Yes, he remembered that she had a child and that he might hurt her, but, as Jay said, this should be about fun.

For them both.

"I have a personal shopper who can get you anything you need."

When she hesitated, he said, "Please. We've both worked so hard, I think we deserve a night." *A night.* Two words that clarified his intentions. She would know what she was agreeing to.

She shook her head. "Okay. But only if I pay for the dress and shoes."

A thrill raced through him. "You don't have to—"

"I do. I always get myself a Christmas gift. So this will be it."

Not giving her a chance to change her mind, he called his personal shopper to tell her Erin would be in touch. When he got off the call, he gave Erin her number. She left his office with his personal shopper's info clutched in her hand.

Even as the joy of getting what he wanted filled him, nerves jumped in his stomach. The whole date had been arranged so simply one would have thought he could settle into work and forget it until time to pick her up at her flat.

But he'd never been so excited about taking

someone to dinner. Never had this shaky feeling over knowing she could be his—all his—for two or three or even four days.

One day at a time. One invitation at a time.

As long as they were having fun. If it ever looked like she was getting serious when he wasn't, he'd know to shut it off.

But he didn't believe it would go that far. Their time together came with a shelf life. Though she was spending Christmas Day in London, he'd be on a plane back to Manhattan. And they wouldn't see each other again for months.

She had to realize that.

CHAPTER EIGHT

EAGER NOW, WISHING the day was over so he could have time with Erin, Hugo bounced out of his seat and walked into what he considered ground central. Things were progressing. Painting done in some places, on target in others.

He saw one of the specialty plasterers and walked over to talk about design. But before they got into their conversation, he saw Sally heading toward him. He'd known she was in the hotel today, but as had been his practice, he let his brother and sister work alone, at their own speed. And while Jay phoned him with updates, Sally still preferred the more impersonal method of emailing.

She looked hesitant walking to him. Then her steps faltered, and he noticed that her color was off. Her face a pasty white.

His chest tightened with fear and he sped up his steps as she reached out her hand. "Hugo!" she said, her knees buckling.

He caught her just as she fell.

An ambulance was called, and Hugo had to fight with the attendant to be able to ride with Sally. But he won. After she was seen by the doctor, he'd waited for her to awaken, but the conversation they'd had hadn't pleased him.

She was pregnant and not intending to marry the baby's father.

Because she wanted to be independent.

The words cut through him like a knife. Not because his little sister had grown up to be strong and capable, but because underlying those words was a worry that having her father die, her older brother desert her and her stepfather cheat her had given her the wrong impression of all men.

Which was why, when he ran into Edward Chen in the Harrington Park lobby on his way out of the hotel to dress for his date with Erin, he almost took the man's head off. He had to be the baby's father. Hugo hadn't seen Sally with anyone else. Not that he saw a lot of her. She rarely told him when she was in the hotel—

But Edward was the guy she'd been staying with when she'd traveled to Tianlipin.

"So? You're just going to drop your responsibilities to my sister?"

Edward gaped at him. Tall and dark-eyed, Edward quietly said, "Drop what responsibilities?"

"To your child!"

Edward eased back a step. "I don't believe this is any of your business."

"Oh, do not kid yourself. My sister and I might not have seen each other for a long time, but she is still my sister and I want to know your intentions."

Edward turned on his heel. "Right now, my intention is to go to the hospital. If you'll excuse me."

With that, he was out the door, and Hugo counted to thirty-five. It wasn't that he didn't believe he had a right to confront Edward. It was more that when Sally found out he'd yelled at her baby's father, she was likely to hit him.

But a weird happiness filled him. His sister was pregnant and no matter who liked it and who didn't, he had held the father accountable.

All right. Edward didn't look like the kind of guy who would abandon his responsibilities. But Hugo had finally been able to step up as big brother again.

Erin stared at the three dresses on the bed. She'd encouraged Hugo's personal shopper to bargain hunt. Though the request had sounded odd to the store managers Kathleen had called, she had found three dresses for about a third of their original cost.

The first was a simple red sheath with a cardigan that could go anywhere. A restaurant or a Christmas party.

The black one was more sleek, sophisticated. That one definitely had Christmas party or gallery opening written all over it.

The blue one was a good dinner choice.

But if Hugo only wanted tonight, she'd be sending back the two dresses she really liked.

Of course, if things went as well as they had the last time she and Hugo were alone…he'd spend every day with her.

Her thoughts drifted back to the night they were stranded at the hotel and eagerness raced through her. When she stopped thinking of things in terms of "permanent," everything was perfect. They laughed. The sex was amazing. And there had been no hurt feelings.

No expectations did that to a person.

She hadn't thought she'd expected too much from her late husband, but maybe she had. And maybe that was the lesson? She wouldn't *attach* herself to anyone who couldn't give her his whole heart and soul, but she could date them. That opened the door to having fun with someone who didn't want to commit, and Hugo was definitely fun.

And probably unable to commit. He hadn't told her much about his life, his family, how they'd become estranged. She'd pieced things together, but he didn't talk, and she was finally beginning to realize that would be for the best, if they were simply together to have fun.

She decided to think positive and slid into the blue dress. It dipped low enough in the front to be alluring, but not so much that it was provocative. Better, though, it brought out the best in her straight red hair. With a little makeup and a pair of black high-heeled pumps, she was ready when the doorbell rang.

She raced to answer it, then forced herself to slow down. Whatever she and Hugo were doing, it was only about fun. A woman only having fun did not race to the door.

The second she opened it, Hugo caught her upper arms and brought her to him for a long, sensual kiss that made her dizzy.

"Wow."

"You're so beautiful."

And just like that, he took an evening that could have started out awkward and brought them both out of work mode and into romance. Happiness tingled through her. *She liked him*. She liked being with him. When there was no discussion, no expectation, no tomorrow guaranteed for them, he was a warm, loving guy.

And from the way his gaze moved from her

face down the lines of her dress, she knew he liked her too.

"I'm going to have to congratulate Kathleen on her choice of outfits."

She almost said, *Just wait. There are two more. Each one better than the last.* But she bit her tongue. There was no guarantee they'd have more than this date. She refused to ruin it by putting him in an odd spot.

She rose on tiptoe to give him a quick kiss. "Thanks."

He took a slow breath. "You're welcome." His gaze rippled down her figure again. "We better get to the limo before I convince you we don't need dinner."

The expression on his face sent her head spinning and arousal careening through her blood. "Maybe we don't."

He laughed. "I'm not starting my third date with you by not feeding you or buying lunch from a vendor the way I did our first and second."

Walking to the limo, she realized he counted their being stuck in the hotel as a date and then him showing her and Noah around as their second, and her heart warmed. Mostly because he liked her son, was easy and casual around her son, like a man who adored children—

Then she reminded herself this was only

about fun, and she pulled herself together. He wanted to wine and dine her. Wasn't that what fun was supposed to be about? Enjoying each other's company, not just falling into bed.

Ronnie opened the limo door. As she entered, Hugo said, "I saw my sister this afternoon."

His simple statement broke the argument in her head. "You did?"

He settled beside her on the long, comfortable seat. "Yes. She fainted in my arms and I called an ambulance."

"I thought I heard scuttlebutt about an ambulance coming to the hotel."

His gaze jumped to hers. "Just scuttlebutt. No out and out gossip?"

"There might have been." She shrugged. "You know me. I don't interrupt the workers unless I need to. Plus, I stay in my own little corner." Cautious because she didn't want to push, she carefully said, "So, what happened?"

"I sort of got to be a big brother."

The pride in his voice made her laugh. "What?"

"It's a complicated situation…and some of it I don't feel comfortable revealing."

"Oh." Confusion jolted through her. Sometimes they were so close, and their conversations seemed so open, that his pulling back was like a bolt of lightning. A hot little sizzle that singed her nerve endings.

"It's about her health." He winced. "Obviously, since she went to the hospital, but suffice to say she's fine. Better than fine. Fit and healthy and probably going home tomorrow."

Erin listened carefully, noting how close he came to telling her something about his family without telling her anything. Still, it was more than he ever said. Even if he was keeping a lot of his life close to the vest, the fact that he'd said anything at all pleased her.

She reminded herself she hadn't entered this relationship to find a husband or even a real boyfriend. She was determined not to be hurt by things he said or didn't say.

"Because the twins are seven years younger than I am, I felt like their protector." He winced. "And by default, something of a teacher. Showing them the ropes about life."

She laughed, warmed again by his sharing with her. "How old were you when you were their guru?"

He thought a second. "I left at seventeen." His head tilted. "So, probably from when I was ten and they were three. At the time I thought I was wise. Turns out I didn't know a damned thing really."

"No seventeen-year-old knows everything."

After laughing with him a bit more about how much he liked being a big brother, they entered the restaurant and she shifted the conversation to something light and friendly. Books they'd read. Movies each had seen—mostly on internet platforms because with his schedule, Hugo didn't go out much.

The way he so casually mentioned it, Erin knew it was true. She desperately tried not to let her brain leap to the conclusion that he didn't have much of a social life, which meant there wasn't a woman waiting for him back in Manhattan—not even a dependable date for social events he needed to attend—and she had to stop that too.

Keeping things light and casual in a relationship didn't happen as naturally as Erin thought it would. Her inclination seemed to be to jump to the future and this wasn't about the future. It was about now.

Still, she liked him. She liked this relaxed version of Hugo who could now trust her with tidbits about his family and converse about simple, mundane things. And dinner was divine. The venue was luxurious and just pretentious enough to demonstrate that she was dating "up" from her own class.

But Hugo never made her feel less than. In fact, he made her feel like the most beautiful woman in the room. Their conversations were filled with intelligence and laughter. Walking out of the restaurant to the limo, warm with wine and happiness, they linked arms.

Ronnie opened the door with a smile and an odd look to Hugo.

Hugo turned her to face him, locking his eyes with hers. "Will you come back to my penthouse with me?"

She didn't hesitate. "Yes."

Ronnie smiled. After they'd entered the limo, he closed the door on them. Cocooning them in the warm, private back seat.

They kissed the entire drive to his building. Kissed in the elevator going up to the penthouse and kissed their way down the hall to the master bedroom. But once they got into the bedroom, both removed their winter coats and he reached for the zipper on her dress.

Abundantly glad she had a fetish for pretty undergarments, she stood still as he peeled away her dress and revealed the pink bra and panties. He kissed her reverently as she loosened his tie and undid the buttons of his white shirt.

He broke their kiss to get rid of his clothes, then rolled her to the bed with him onto silk sheets that slid sensuously against her skin. Her breathing slowed, even as her thoughts jumped to double time, taking it all in. The fierceness of his kiss, the solidness of his muscles beneath her palms. She wanted to remember every little detail for cold Manhattan nights, if only because this was a temporary fling.

But her brain shut down when his fingers skimmed her flesh and his mouth found her breast. Her breathing stuttered as heat and need flowed through her veins, pooling at a point just below her belly. What started out slow and easy quickly heated to boiling. Their joining was swift and intense. Kisses became hot and desperate. Until a stunning climax roared through her and she felt his follow.

For a few seconds she simply let herself breathe. Then he raised himself to smile down into her eyes, and something inside her heart cracked and opened. But she caught it just in time, before those haunted gray eyes of his could soften her to the point that she felt things she knew she wasn't allowed to feel.

The emotions were there, right on the surface, and she longed to indulge them. Instead, she ignored them.

She wouldn't let herself fall for another man with secrets. Though he might not have realized it, he'd drawn a line that day by only taking her so far into his confidence about his sister.

But remembering that would keep her from getting her heart broken and help her to simply enjoy what they had.

* * *

She woke the next morning so sated and happy that she decided to make him breakfast in bed. In a relationship that was only about fun, there was no room for second-guessing her every move. There was no way she could be too forward. No worry that she'd scare him off and there'd be no more dates. She had no idea if he'd want to see her that night, if he'd chase her home so he could get some work done this morning or if they'd spend the day—Sunday—together. She also didn't care.

A little voice inside her brain said that wasn't true, but she shoved it aside. She and Hugo were not a match made in heaven. Even if he somehow gave her the magical sign that she meant something to him, she should be smart enough to give returning his feelings a lot of thought. He was a man with secrets and an odd past. A smart woman wouldn't want to get involved with that. At least not permanently. So right now, she had no expectations. She liked him. She loved talking with him and he was a fabulous lover whose generosity made her a better lover because she wasn't afraid of messing up what they had. They had nothing. Except that moment.

Having no expectations was a beautiful thing. With bacon frying on the stove and bagels in the toaster, Erin had her back to the open area of the penthouse when Hugo walked up behind her, slid his arms around her waist and kissed her neck.

She laughed. "You better step back or you'll get splashed with bacon grease."

"I have a robe on...since someone stole my shirt."

She winced. "Sorry, didn't want to put on my new dress to cook bacon."

He nibbled the back of her neck. "I like you in my shirt... I like you better in my bed."

"After we eat. Last night was amazing, but we drained every drop of energy I have. We need to power up."

"Good thinking." He slid away from her. "Anything I can do?"

"Nope. I only found bacon, cream cheese and bagels. No eggs. So maybe bacon sandwiches?"

"Sounds great."

"Get some plates and napkins while I take the bacon out of the pan and we'll be set."

He did what he was told but when they sat at the breakfast bar, they both got quiet. After a few bites of bagel, he said, "So you weren't upset about your mum taking your son and running away to Ireland?"

She laughed, licking some cream cheese off her thumb. He might not be able to tell her much about himself, but her life was not a secret. She had no qualms telling him anything.

"No. My mom has never had extended family around. Since my parents' divorce, my mom's been pretty much alone. Except for me. I got married and my husband died before I had Noah. So, though we have a Noah, who we didn't have before, my mom and I are back to being pretty much alone."

"Where's your dad?"

She shrugged. "Don't know. I invited him to my wedding, but he declined. Luckily, by that point my mom and I didn't care. I was so thrilled to be marrying Josh that having my dad refuse to walk me down the aisle just made room for my mom to do it."

Erin glanced down at her bacon when she said her husband's name, and Hugo fought a battle with jealousy. The man was gone, but it was clear there was still a boatload of emotion there.

He wanted to ask what the man—Josh—was like. What he'd done for a living. How he'd died. Partly out of curiosity. Partly because he longed to find a rift, a flaw, something he could identify and use to make the jealousy go away.

But he reminded himself that his relationship with Erin was a temporary thing. And hearing Erin say her husband had died, her dad had de-

serted her, her mum and son were her only people, he knew she needed some fun in her life.

Maybe more than he did. And maybe he was looking at this relationship all wrong. It might be casual, but that didn't mean they couldn't share their troubles. Their lives had a few similarities and it wouldn't hurt to admit that.

He took a breath. "Your mum's obsession with finding her Irish relatives reminds me of me trying to get my family back together."

Her gaze jumped to his. He understood why. He'd never really said those words to anyone. She might have guessed. He might have hinted. But he'd never actually come right out and said it.

"I think it's a biological imperative to be connected."

She bobbed her head. "I suppose."

"And while she fulfills that need and hopefully really does find her roots, her place—" he leaned in and wrapped his arms around her waist "—you and I can enjoy ourselves."

Her smile was quick and genuine. "What do you have in mind?"

"A sightseeing tour."

Her eyes widened. "Really?"

"The adult version."

Her eyes widened even more, and he laughed. "I don't mean sex on the lawn of Buckingham

Palace. I mean there won't be any stops to see Santa."

She laughed. "Whew. I'm okay with being adventurous, but I don't want to be arrested in a foreign country."

This time he laughed. Long and loud. In a way he couldn't remember laughing for a long time. His sister was okay. Pregnant. But okay. He'd got to be a big brother the day before. And the woman he desired was at his fingertips. Not just for bed, but to really enjoy the day.

"The limo will have to take me back to my apartment to dress."

He rose from his stool by the breakfast bar. "Sounds good. I'll call Ronnie, get a shower and dress. Then we'll drive to your apartment."

He kissed her quickly. "Your phone's in the master bedroom. So's the shower. You could come back there with me for some really adult fun before I clean up. Then you might want to give your mum and Noah a call."

She smiled. "Sounds perfect."

CHAPTER NINE

IT *WAS* PERFECT. All of it. The drive through London gave her a real feel for the city. The stops at Buckingham Palace for a closer look and the Thames Path—Hampton Court to Albert Bridge—were especially nice. A late lunch at an out-of-the-way bistro ended their outing and they returned to her flat for her to change again.

It seemed oddly foolish to keep stopping at her home to grab her things for the quiet evening in his penthouse that they'd agreed to, but the alternative was for him to say, *Just pack a bag*, and he wasn't sure what message that would send.

When she came out to the apartment's main room, her overnight case in hand, she walked to him, rose on tiptoe and kissed him. "Let's go."

And he suddenly didn't care what kind of message it sent, except by the time he thought to suggest she get more clothes, she was already in the hall.

They returned to his penthouse to find Louis Joubert and his staff working in the kitchen.

She turned to him with a smile. "What's this?"

"A special dinner."

"Thought we were going to have a quiet evening?"

"This is quiet. He's going to let us sample Christmas Eve dinner."

She faced Louis. "How nice."

"It never hurts to be sure the boss is pleased with your creation," Louis said.

Hugo laughed. "Jay chose you. I know how picky he is. Which means I also know you'll be phenomenal."

"And you'll get to tell me so, once you taste the goose."

An hour later, Hugo and Erin sat down to a dinner of goose, ham and chocolate mousse, with side dishes of mashed potatoes and green beans almandine, as well as hot rolls.

"There'll also be chocolate cake, if anyone dislikes mousse," Louis said, when he came in for a final bow at the end of the meal.

Erin said, "It was amazing. All of it."

"Absolutely perfect," Hugo agreed.

Louis took his bow, then exited the dining area. Hugo and Erin retired to the living room where they watched a movie on the large-screen

TV, as Louis and his staff cleaned the kitchen and gathered their things.

But as they filed out of the penthouse, Hugo's phone rang. Recognizing Jay's number, he answered. "Jay. What's up?"

"Where have you been? I've been trying to reach you all day."

He winced. "I had my phone off because I took Erin sightseeing. Why?"

"It's Sally. She was at the hospital yesterday."

"I know. I'm the one went with her in the ambulance."

"You did?"

Hugo sat back. "Did she tell you she was pregnant? I had to have a word with the baby's father. I hope he steps up like he promised."

"Did you know he's wealthy?"

"Neither of them told me that. But it doesn't matter how much money he has. No man should desert a woman he got pregnant."

"Don't get your knickers in a twist. Sally told me today that they're getting married."

Hugo sat up. "Married?"

"Yes."

"That's great news. If that's what she wants."

"You're sounding a little too proud."

Feeling like his big brother speech had hit home, Hugo laughed. "I'm relieved my intervention helped."

"You must not have done any damage if they got engaged."

"Or maybe I can take credit."

Jay laughed. "Don't go that far."

"Sure. Fine. Whatever. But if I get invited to the wedding, I'm taking credit in a dinner toast."

Jay laughed again and they said their goodbyes.

As he tossed his phone to the end table beside the sofa, Erin slid her arm beneath his and nestled against him. "So, your sister is pregnant?"

He grimaced. "Yeah."

"And you feel like you had a hand in your future brother-in-law's proposal?"

He laughed. "He came to the hotel yesterday looking for her and I didn't hold back."

She sat up. "The intervention you told Jay about?"

"Yes. I told him I didn't think very much of a guy who gets a woman pregnant and deserts her." He grinned. "Then he proposed. You don't think that was my doing?"

She shook her head. "You *really* enjoy being a big brother."

"Yeah," he said with another grin, but he quickly sobered. "But, honestly, with all the lost years between us, I don't have a clue what I'm doing."

"Well, this time, you did great." She snorted

a laugh. "In an odd kind of way, your yelling at the guy proves to Sally you'll be there for her. And maybe that's all she needed to hear."

"I'm not even sure he would have told her. For all I know, he went into her hospital room and proposed as if it were his idea."

She arched a brow. "Maybe it was."

Proud, he sat up. "I'm taking credit."

"Yeah, I can see that. But it looks to me like you needed that confrontation more than their relationship did."

"*I* did?"

"Yes." Her eyes were soft and serious as she added, "It's proof of how much you still want to be a big brother. Plus, that's how people step into a role they aren't sure of. They say and do the right thing over and over until it's part of their life. You haven't defended your sister before, so yesterday it was new. If you guys ever get your troubles straightened out, you're already one step into the game."

He studied her face, realizing not just how much he'd told her about himself with a few throwaway comments, but how well she listened—how much she cared. "You're awfully smart for someone so young."

She laughed. "I'm not that young." She took a breath. "I've also had some hard lessons."

He knew she had, and said nothing for a few

seconds, but in the silence, all of Hugo's questions about her husband came pouring back and he couldn't stop them. "Because of losing your husband?"

"Yes." She took another breath, this one much longer as if she were debating telling him anything about her past. He supposed he deserved it, but the itchy feeling wouldn't go away. He desperately wanted to know about the man who had won her heart.

"I imagine losing your spouse is the worst thing in the world."

"It is. But in my case, not for the reasons you think."

Confusion brought him up short. "You weren't sad when he died?"

"I was devastated when he died. The devastation was made worse when I discovered he'd been sick for a while and had been getting experimental treatments for terminal cancer."

"Terminal cancer?" Hugo's stomach fell. "But you made it sound like you didn't know he was sick."

"I didn't. He was only getting treatments for a few weeks before they weakened his heart, and he had a heart attack and died. Knowing what was coming, he'd shaved his head, telling me it was the style. When he lost weight, he told me he'd joined a gym."

Concern for her squeezed his lungs, his heart, even as confusion almost rendered him speechless. "Why didn't he tell you?"

"He claimed he'd done it to spare me. Because I was pregnant, he didn't want me to worry about his health too."

"That makes a weird kind of sense…"

"But you don't think it was right, do you?"

When he didn't answer—was so flabbergasted he didn't know what to think, let alone say—she shook her head.

"Marriage is a partnership. It's like your hotel investments. You commit to certain things but when you begin a project, you have no idea what kinds of problems will be thrown at you."

"I have some idea because I do a great deal of investigating before I make any commitments."

"But there are no guarantees you won't find something unexpected."

"There are never any guarantees."

"Marriage is the same. You go into it with a plan, expectations, then things happen. People lose jobs. Houses are difficult to find and afford—all kinds of things. In our case, Josh got sick when I was pregnant."

"But didn't tell you. So you couldn't fulfill your end of the bargain and it hurt you."

"Yes. But it was more. I didn't find out he needed me until he was already dead. Do you know how guilty that made me feel? And how much worse I felt when I discovered there was someone he confided in?"

"Please tell me it wasn't another woman."

"It was. She was a coworker. My mother believes he needed someone to talk to or someone to help with his workload and he turned to someone he could trust."

He realized how isolated they were and how the darkness of the room must have either made her bold or comfortable. So he spoke his mind. "And that was the real betrayal. In finding someone else, he all but said he didn't trust you."

"That's what I felt. And that's why I understand the importance of trust. Of saying and doing what you're supposed to be saying and doing. Josh might have believed it was the worst time in the world to be sick. Especially since my pregnancy was difficult. But that didn't change the fact that he was terminally ill. He robbed us of the opportunity to face it together, to make videos for his son… Most of all he robbed me of a voice in his decision to try an experimental treatment."

"I understand." He did. "My stepdad—Nick—robbed me of almost two decades of time with my siblings. I missed my own mother's funeral because no one told me she'd died."

"I'm so sorry."

He shook his head. Erin not being trusted by her husband mirrored his not being wanted by his family. The pain of it wasn't a big, angry wound. It was a huge, open hole that he didn't know what to do with.

That Erin didn't know what to do with.

Empty Christmases. Solitary birthdays. Blank spaces where people should have been. True, Erin had her mum and son, but in some ways, he wondered if that didn't make her husband's loss more obvious.

"The thing is, I don't merely understand your loss. I kind of understand why your husband didn't tell you. I kept some secrets." He took a breath. "I should have told my mum the very first time I suspected Nick was embezzling."

"He embezzled?"

"Yes, and blamed me." He ran his hand along the back of his neck. "I don't want to get into all of it, but I do understand why your husband didn't tell you. When you love someone that much, it's like you'd give your life to keep them safe." He pictured Erin pregnant, enduring difficulties. Then he put himself in the place of the man he didn't know and easily recognized why he'd believed he couldn't tell her.

"He was sheltering you. Trying to protect you while he fought a battle to save his own life."

She studied his face. "You make it sound very noble."

"To him it was."

"I guess I never really tried to see his side."

"You should."

She leaned back on the sofa again. Her shoulder brushed his and confusion flooded his brain.

Now that he understood her husband, it seemed callous to be taking his widow back to his bedroom to have meaningless sex.

But he thought again about those gaping holes in her life. Because he knew them too. Understood the empty places where people should have been. Understood the sorrow that overshadowed holidays.

He swore he wasn't using her. *Knew* he wasn't using her—

Because they were having fun. *She* was having fun.

And it sounded like she needed it.

Still, he took his time easing them into the rest of their night. They drank wine, talked a little more, and kissed slowly, easily. He had absolutely no idea what he was doing, except Erin was a wonderful woman...a wonderful person. He had been privileged to spend time with her and if it killed him he would make sure their being together filled up her empty places, shored up her defenses and warmed her with the knowledge that she was special and wonderful. So that when she was ready to find a real relationship, she would have the confidence of a Greek goddess.

Even though they went to work on Monday, Erin had the odd sense that they were on their honeymoon. Sightseeing? Romantic dinners? Long, meaningful talks? Sex every time they were alone? That was a honeymoon.

She could confess that to Hugo, and he'd break the spell with hard truths, hard reality. Then she'd get her thoughts straightened out. But she couldn't do it. Something had changed after he'd taken Sally to the hospital or maybe after she'd told Hugo about Josh and Hugo had understood—helped *her* to understand. She hadn't meant to so easily spill her big secret. She'd meant to show him that there were many ways people could betray each other, hurt each other. And she had. But telling that one small truth had also brought them closer—

After he'd admitted to yelling at the father of Sally's child and let her see that he was inordinately proud.

He'd let her see. He'd let her in.

So she'd let him in.

Now she had no idea what they were doing. Making love really had become making love the night before. The things they'd done, the way they'd kissed had formed some kind of connection. They'd bonded.

They'd bonded.

Her heart jolted with fear.

Oh, God. Now, she would be so hurt when this ended!

Except, after their discussion, it didn't feel like it was going to end. Which should have scared her silly. Bonded to a man whose past she didn't understand? A man who still had secrets?

It was exactly what she didn't want.

But every time he looked her in the eye when he listened, every time he took her in his arms and kissed her—

Nothing had ever felt more right.

"So, you're looking bright and chipper!"

Marge's voice interrupted her thoughts. After her mom called saying she and Noah were returning, Hugo had arranged for Ronnie to drive Erin to the airport to pick them up. With Noah strapped into the car seat Hugo had bought and her mom right beside her, Erin couldn't evade the implied question.

"I had a nice weekend."

"Re-e-all-y…"

"Mom. Stop. Seriously."

"Well, if you don't want to talk about Hugo—"

"What makes you think my mood has anything to do with Hugo?"

Her mother blinked. "What else could it be? You light up like a Christmas tree when he's around. But today, even though he's not here, your cheeks are pink. And there's something about your posture..." Her mom gave her a quick once-over. "It wasn't that you slouched before." She snapped her fingers. "I know. You were too stiff. Now you're sitting straight and tall, but in a relaxed way."

Erin gaped at her. "What?"

"I don't know." Marge shrugged. "You're normal. Back to normal."

"Normal as compared to what?"

"The woman who had to have a child alone because she believed her husband betrayed her." Marge studied her face. "Have you forgiven Josh?"

Erin pulled her fingers through her hair. But when she tried to say no, or to tell her mom it was irrelevant, she realized she *had* forgiven Josh. Somewhere, somehow in spilling her guts to Hugo and having him explain why Josh had kept his secret, she'd let it all go.

Her heart expanded and filled her chest. Having Hugo identify with Josh had eased her into looking at her past, and she had seen Josh as Josh. Not blinded by her own needs, her own hurts, she understood his fears. But also, hearing Hugo talk about his family, and seeing his fight to bring them back together, she understood Josh's sense of responsibility. Just as Hugo was now putting his own feelings aside, Josh had ruthlessly put his feelings aside—

Her head spun. She had finally gotten beyond it. And she had Hugo to thank.

Grumpy Hugo Harrington.

No...*wounded* Hugo Harrington.

"Are you okay?"

"Yeah, Mom. I'm fine. I'm just finally seeing Josh's side of things."

Her mom's eyes narrowed. "Really?"

"I did spend time with Hugo while you were gone. He told me he went to the hospital with his sister, who is pregnant. He was so thrilled to get to play the part of big brother for her that it was amazing. He never said it, but he put his own needs aside, his own questions about what happened when he and his siblings were younger, and just reacted, protecting his sister."

"That's lovely." Her mom's voice was soft, compassionate.

Erin smiled. "He's had a rough life."

"Hugo or Josh?"

"Both, I guess. They are nothing alike. But they have a sense of responsibility and some sort of weird male pride that makes them think they are in charge of everything. I saw Josh through Hugo. Trying to spare everybody by taking on all the burden himself."

"What about him telling the other woman?"

She licked her lips. "Everybody has a breaking point." She didn't tell her mom that she suddenly realized she was "the woman to confide in" in Hugo's story. No matter how wonderful their time together, she knew he'd hit his breaking point the day they went into the attic to look at decorations. She'd forced him into a corner, and he'd decided they should leave the office— go for hot cocoa. But she'd set up the scenario.

Josh's female friend had sworn that Josh had simply needed a release valve, someone to talk to, and now Erin totally understood that. Even as forgiveness for Josh filled her soul and gave her peace, her relationship with Hugo came into perspective.

While she was worrying that she was falling in love, he was working out his past, probably appreciating that he could drop a tidbit here and there and not fear that she would judge, because she'd endured hardship too.

He might never explain the whole of it, but he was talking to her. She would always be the woman who helped him through the hardest days of his life, but he would never love her. She would always remind him of his terrible past.

Even if she was the person who helped him fix it.

This wasn't the beginning of something wonderful. It was the end of something horrible for Hugo.

And if it was the beginning of anything, it was a heartache for her.

CHAPTER TEN

WHEN RONNIE RETURNED Erin to the Harrington Park Hotel, Hugo stood at the door, waiting for her.

"How was their trip?"

She looked up at him, her gaze locking with his for a few seconds as she stared into his eyes. Then she glanced away. "Good. She loves everybody. Had it not been for Noah getting cranky, missing me, I think she could have stayed forever."

Feeling as if something was off, but not able to identify it, Hugo carefully said, "That's good, right?"

"Yeah. Sure." She sighed and shook her head. "Actually, it's excellent. I know how she's longed for her family, and you bringing us here gave her a chance we never would have had without you, if only because we couldn't afford it."

He casually put his arm around her, feeling, for some reason or another, that she needed reassurance. "Nonsense, you're the best. Some day your business is going to really take off and you're going to be the 'it' girl for events in Manhattan."

She smiled, but the smile didn't reach her eyes. "That'll be great."

What she said was good, but like her eyes, her voice didn't back up the sentiment of it. Not knowing what to do, he left her, veering off when they reached his office. But sitting at his desk, reading progress reports, the feeling that he had to fix this overtook him. He didn't like that something was troubling Erin. He also realized that with her mum and son home, they wouldn't sleep together tonight. His big bed would be cold and lonely, but this feeling he had wasn't about him.

Erin was off. She couldn't be unhappy. Her son was home. She'd probably hugged and kissed him a million times.

So, what the hell was it?

After an hour of contemplation, he was still stymied. He couldn't stand the thought that something was wrong and shoved himself out of his desk chair and headed to the kitchen, where he instructed Louis to send up a sample tray of everything he and his staff had created that day. Then he called Erin and told her to meet him in the penthouse.

When the elevator opened for her to enter, the little penthouse kitchen was filled with everything from lobster to pudding.

She sniffed the air and groaned with pleasure. "What's all this?"

"Food to sample. Louis doesn't just have to feed a hotel filled with guests on Christmas Eve. He's got to make breakfasts, lunches and dinners for their entire stays." He motioned to the counter lined with samples. "What you see right here is him trying to pin down his restaurant menu."

She walked over and sniffed the air. "And we're the guinea pigs?"

He laughed. "Or you could say we're the lucky people who get to taste test." He picked up a bit of lobster, dipped it in butter and popped it in his mouth. "The man is a genius."

She laughed. "And we're both going to have to join a gym when we get back to Manhattan—" Her breath caught slightly.

And Hugo knew why. Mentioning Manhattan shoved them back to reality, back to being a businessman and the woman he employed to plan his events.

Even as his heart jolted at the thought of not seeing her after this wonderful affair, he wondered if they really did have to part. Maybe what had started out as an affair had turned into something solid? Something real?

Maybe that was what she was feeling? The confusion of a temporary arrangement edging over into something permanent.

It should have scared him. He'd never believed he was the kind of guy who'd find love. He didn't think he had time for love or a big enough place in his life. But what he experienced with her was so different, so important, it filled his heart.

The shock of it should have made him at least pause and consider the consequences. Instead, the longing he'd been battling since she'd arrived in London had him patting the stool beside his. Taking a chance. "Sit."

With a nervous laugh, she did as he said.

But the laugh confirmed his suspicions. She'd never been nervous around him before. Recognizing that, he concluded the shift in their situation had to be the problem. Still, he didn't have any answers. He was as baffled as she was.

There was only one way to handle this. Just keep doing what they'd been doing—enjoying each other's company—and see what happened.

"Why don't we play a food game? You close your eyes and I'll feed you a bite of something and you try to guess what it is."

She rolled her eyes. "Hugo…really…"

"Close your eyes."

Skeptical, she nonetheless closed her eyes. Using a slim seafood fork, he took a piece of lobster, dipped it in butter and said, "Open your mouth."

She opened her mouth and he set the lobster on her tongue.

She groaned with pleasure. "Mmm...lobster."

"That one was easy." He paused. "You've got a little butter on your mouth." He leaned in, kissed it away.

Her eyes opened and she smiled. Hugo's chest filled. He'd hated to see her sad, and in ten minutes he'd brought his Erin back.

"Close your eyes again. I don't want you peeping."

She laughed. He chose a small bite of filet mignon. "Open your mouth."

She shook her head, fanning her beautiful red hair along her shoulders, but opened her mouth, and he set the filet on her tongue.

"Oh, God, that's good. Perfect."

"Louis is a genius."

Her eyelids lifted and again she smiled. "So you've said."

He leaned in. "I think I see sauce on your lips."

"There was no sauce on the steak..." She stopped when his lips met hers. This time he put his arm around her waist, pulling her close, deepening the kiss.

He'd never felt so powerful or so happy that he could make someone smile. He enticed her nearer and nearer until she was on his lap. Then he kissed them both into oblivion, as he removed her T-shirt and she got rid of his jacket and tie.

He could have taken her right there in the kitchen, but with elevator doors that could open for anyone who had the code, he decided against that and drew her back to the bedroom with him.

After they made love, she fell asleep beside him, and that indescribable joy filled him again. The thought that he had found his place, his purpose, tiptoed through his brain, and for once he didn't argue.

The beep of his phone floated back from the main living area, interrupting his thoughts. He eased out of bed, careful not to wake Erin as he slipped into his shirt and pants. He couldn't believe he'd got so involved that he didn't realize he'd left his phone behind and shook his head at the strength of whatever it was between him and Erin.

He grabbed a bite of watermelon from the fruit salad Louis had prepared and walked to the coffee table, where he'd left his phone. He hit a button and saw eight missed calls.

Eight missed calls?

And one voice mail.

"Hey, Hugo. Not sure what's going on, but Sally's gone back to Tianlipin. She'd thought you might have come to the hospital when she was released on Sunday and was surprised you hadn't." There was a pause, and then Jay added, "It's odd. It's as if she expects to see you now and again."

Hugo's heart stopped and he fell to the sofa in the seating area. Sally had talked about him? Expected to see him?

He slammed his phone on the sofa cushion with an unsatisfying thud and bounced up to pace, his thoughts going a million miles a second. Then he realized he'd been showing Erin around London on Sunday. He'd never followed up with Sally about her hospital stay because Jay had called him and given him a report.

He hadn't given Sally a passing thought.

He bent and grabbed the phone again, calling Jay. "It never entered my mind to see her off on Sunday."

Jay laughed. "No biggie."

But it was a biggie to Hugo. A door had opened—

No. He'd opened a door by taking Sally to

the hospital, talking to her, yelling at her now-fiancé, and then he'd forgotten about it.

"I wasn't there either. She'd called telling me she was home. I'm assuming that's Tianlipin. Look. Don't make too much of this."

Easy for Jay to say. He wasn't the one on the outside looking in. Hoping for an opening. Praying for a way to show Sally his intentions were genuine and that he'd spent years missing her and Jay.

He'd found it, and then he'd walked away.

Still, he wouldn't let Jay see his annoyance with himself. "Okay. Fine. Whatever."

Erin strolled out of the bedroom, saw he was on the phone and motioned to the center island still filled with Louis's goodies.

He watched the gentle sway of her hips and his mouth watered, the way it did every time he looked at her.

He told himself not to make too much of that either. Though he'd had all kinds of thoughts of permanency with her, those couldn't be real. Not when he had so much else on his mind. He was in the middle of trying to renovate his family's hotel and reconcile with his brother and sister…he didn't have the mental energy left to get involved with a woman.

Which was the entire state of his life. Strong feelings or not, he was a ridiculously busy man.

He could have fun with her, yes. But when they returned to Manhattan his life would get crazy again. Hotels would go up for sale. His brand would need reinforcing. And if he was lucky, his brother and sister would want him in their world.

Those were the things he'd worked his entire life for.

Those were his goals.

The things that had filled him with purpose and kept him from sinking into a black pit of despair after his mum had kicked him out.

He couldn't abandon them because of a few days. Especially since Erin's odd mood might have been because she was also recognizing their time together was ending.

He finished the call with Jay, went back to the food and stayed in the moment as he and Erin ate lunch.

He reminded himself that this wasn't a relationship. It was fun. And those thoughts he'd had when he'd called her to come up to the penthouse? They were foolish musings of a guy having a really great time with a very special woman. She was sad. He wanted to make her happy. Because that was what their relationship was about. Fun. Nothing more.

When she left the penthouse to go back to

work, he returned to the office with his New York staff.

He didn't wonder if she'd got home safely. At the end of her workday, he sent the limo to take her to her flat. But he didn't call to see how she was. Didn't go to the hotel first thing in the morning. He went back to the office with his staff, where he belonged.

Moving boxes was not how Erin had intended to spend her Wednesday morning, but with her workstation now overtaken by the painters, she had no choice. The mountains of paperwork on the desk Hugo used when he was in the hotel prevented her from usurping that area. So she'd had some workmen bring her small desk downstairs into Hugo's office, but they'd dropped it in the middle of everything.

She shoved boxes against the walls, carving out a place where she could push the desk, and was thrilled when she had everything arranged. But a box fell off the old-fashioned filing cabinet and dumped its contents all over the floor.

"Stupid clutter!" She crouched to pick up the papers, file folders and envelopes scattered around. She knew she was out of sorts because her time with Hugo continually confused her. She shouldn't like him, shouldn't enjoy his company, but lately he'd been damned near irresistible, baffling her. Making her long for things she couldn't have because as soon as they returned to Manhattan, he'd associate her with trouble, not success. And he wouldn't want to see her anymore.

She almost launched the papers and file folders across the room, if only to get them out of the way. "Why do people save everything?"

But when she saw Sally Harrington neatly printed on the front of one of the red envelopes and Hugo Harrington's name in the space for the return address, she stopped cold.

She looked at the postal stamp cancellation to see the date, then rifled through at least twenty dusty red and green envelopes—probably Christmas cards—with Hugo's return address, mailed to James and Sally. *His brother and sister.*

Gobsmacked, she sat on the cluttered floor. He'd tried to get in touch with his brother and sister, but the cards had never gotten to the twins. Someone had held them back.

More secrets.

Her heart stuttered. She'd never had the feelings for another person that she had for Hugo Harrington. He was sweet, caring, and more fun-loving than she'd ever expected him to be. He'd sensed her mood the day before and dispelled all her fears, and dear God in heaven, she was falling for him—

Had fallen for him.

She loved him. Loved a man who would undoubtedly dump her when they returned to New York. Loved a man with secrets. And in her hand, she held another one. He'd tried to stay in touch.

She blew the dust off one of the green cards, staring at it as if expecting it to give her the answer. In a way, it did. Whoever hid the cards might not have wanted Sally and Jay to have them, but he or she hadn't been able to toss them away either.

His mother?

Most likely. The stepfather who'd brought their hotel to ruins wouldn't have been sentimental enough to keep them. But a mom trying to protect the twins from whatever Hugo might have said? She'd keep the cards. She might not have had courage enough to open them, but she clearly wanted the connection to Hugo and might have even hoped something good was inside. So, though she hadn't summoned the nerve to open them, she'd kept them.

Erin stared at the small stack of cards, sadness permeating her soul. If Hugo had wanted to leave his family, had wanted his freedom, wanted the clean break, would he have tried to keep in touch?

Probably not.

The only conclusion that could be drawn from Hugo reaching out was that he had wanted to stay connected. And if he had wanted to stay connected, was it so far-fetched to believe that he might not have wanted to leave at all?

Did that explain why he'd bought this hotel—*waited* to buy this hotel?

And if he hadn't wanted to leave, it had to have been his stepfather who'd pushed him out. A mother unable to part with cards from her son couldn't have been the one to shove him out. But a stepfather who didn't want an older child around, a child smart enough to remember the past and strong enough to make his wishes known, would definitely kick him to the curb. Especially since Hugo had said he'd caught his stepfather embezzling.

Poor Hugo!

Her heart squeezed. But she took a breath. She was only making assumptions.

She stared at the dusty envelopes. As an employee, it was none of her business. As his lover? He hadn't told her the whole story of his past, but he'd told her enough that she knew she had to show him these cards.

She shoved them into the big manila envelope, set it on top of a filing cabinet and went back to work.

Twenty minutes later, she had her desk arranged. Her head down, she focused on last-minute details for the big Christmas Eve celebration, especially deliveries. Food was arriving now. Chefs were reconciling the purchase orders against packing slips, but so was she. Everything was checked and double-checked.

"Knock! Knock!"

Erin glanced up to see her mom at the door, sliding Noah to the floor. He ran to her. "Mum!"

Erin laughed as she hoisted him into her arms. "Since when do you call me Mum?"

Her mom sauntered in. "He's been picking up the language subtleties like a little parrot."

She pulled his cap off his head and smoothed his static-filled red hair before he bounced off her lap to explore the office. "What brings you here?"

Marge said, "I have an errand and can't take Noah." She winced. "I was hoping you could keep him for a few hours."

Rising from her seat, she hesitated. Pretending the envelope of Hugo's Christmas cards was no big deal, she slid it off the filing cabinet and into the empty top drawer. Everything was too chaotic to show them to Hugo today. Or worse,

for him to find them. She should probably wait
until after the holiday—

No. Hugo being able to show these cards to
his brother and sister might be the thing that
helped Sally and Jay see he'd been forced out
of their lives. She had to do it today...or maybe
tonight? Maybe she could entice *him* up to the
penthouse before she went home?

"Can you keep him? I swear I won't be long."

Pulled out of her reverie, she turned her attention to her mom again.

Though most construction had been finished,
the hotel was a beehive of activity and everyone
was tense. It might not be a good idea to have
Noah underfoot.

But when her little boy smiled at her, with his
baby teeth all in a straight white row and his
blue eyes gleaming, she ruffled his hair. "Sure.
Why not?"

"Why not what?" Hugo asked, walking past
her mom to come into the office. He stopped
short when he saw her desk. "What's this?"

"They're painting my office. I got the workmen to bring my desk down here. I don't want
to mess up any of the clean spaces. And if I go
to another room that's in line to be painted, I'll
just be moving again."

He grunted. "Good point."

Her mom said, "So it's okay if Noah stays?"

Hugo pivoted to face Marge. "What?"

Before her mom could speak, Erin quickly said, "I was just getting settled when my mom came with Noah and asked if I could keep him for a few hours."

Fear had her heart beating so fast she almost couldn't breathe. Up to now, she hadn't thought too much about whether Hugo liked Noah. Now, suddenly, it was the most important thing in the world.

Hugo surprised her. "Actually, that might be a good idea. There are a few things I'd like to see a child's reaction to."

Erin's lungs filled with air again. "Really?"

"Sure." He smiled at Marge. "You go. He'll be fine here."

With a kiss on Noah's cheek, Marge scampered off.

Hugo stooped in front of Noah. "You remember me, right?"

Noah nodded.

"I'm going to show you something really special. Will you come with me?"

He nodded eagerly.

Hands on Noah's waist, Hugo lifted him as he rose. "I want to see his reaction to the courtyard garden."

"Sure," Erin said, so confused she would have liked to sit again. It almost seemed like the guy she knew in Manhattan was gone. The man she'd thought had a heart of stone had taken to her son as if he loved him. He'd sent cards to his brother and sister that were never delivered. He was good to her mom…and to her. Very, very good to her.

Her heart stumbled with hope.

Maybe it hadn't been a mistake to fall in love with him?

CHAPTER ELEVEN

THEY MADE THEIR way to the ballroom, Hugo holding Noah and Noah giggling with excitement.

He glanced down at the little boy and the strangest feelings rippled through him. This little boy needed a father. Another reason for him to make sure he backed off his relationship with Erin when they returned to Manhattan. If something serious ever happened between him and Erin, he would be Noah's stepfather.

His breath stuttered. He'd had the *worst* example of a stepfather imaginable.

Of course, that could mean he knew what not to do.

He shook his head, telling himself these thoughts were pointless. He wasn't made for a family. He was a businessman. Someone who worked at all hours of the night if he had to. Plus, his goal of getting his family together was in reach.

He couldn't divide his attention and miss that opportunity. Jay's call on Monday had shown him how easily his own family could slip through his fingers. His goals could turn to dust. The hole in his heart could remain cold and barren simply because he lost focus.

They walked through the clean space, newly painted, floors redone and round tables being set up around the dance floor. When the doors opened on to the garden, his breath stalled. Plants that had been put into place fully grown were dewy from the mist that spritzed down on them every morning. A miniforest with fir trees, winterberry shrubs and snow surrounded a skating rink that looked like a frozen lake. Tiles created walkways between the plants and two sections had been arranged: the skating rink and the area housing Santa's throne.

His lungs couldn't seem to fill. It would be the perfect addition to the Christmas Eve launch party for the restored Harrington Park.

"Do you see that chair over there?" he said to Noah, pointing across the garden. "That's actually a throne."

Noah only looked at him, waiting for more information.

Their eyes locked for a few seconds and a strange connection began to form. It was as if the little boy was checking him out to see if he was worthy of liking.

Finally, Hugo said, "Because he's so special, Santa sits on a throne."

Noah gasped. "Santa?"

The little squeal broke the spell of connection. Hugo wondered if he'd imagined it, but he also got the feeling he'd just scored major points with Noah. "Yes. Santa will be here."

Noah squirmed to be put down and Hugo lowered him to the floor. He scampered over to the throne, a tall-backed chair with a red velvet seat and trimmed with gold paint.

Catching Hugo's gaze, Noah said, "I saw Santa."

"I know. I was with you, remember?"

"Noah also saw him in Ireland." Erin walked over to the throne. "I think he's confused because he's already seen him twice, and I'm sure Irish Santa spoke with an accent."

Connection wove around and through them. Him to Erin. Erin to Noah. Noah back to Hugo again. It was almost as rich and deep as the feelings he'd had around his family when his father had been alive. He blamed it on the space. The throne they were using for Santa had been around since his father had planned the Christmas Eve event.

He cautiously answered Erin. "I'm sure he did have a bit of a brogue."

Erin stooped in front of Noah. "Santa can be many places." She winced and faced Hugo again. "Won't the kids wonder what Santa's doing at the hotel when he's supposed to be delivering presents?"

"My dad always told them that he didn't start his rounds until midnight. Then our Santa would make a big deal out of leaving. He'd wave and say he had lots of work to do and every kid in the room would get big-eyed with anticipation."

He could see it in his mind, feel the excitement from all those years ago, but with Erin and Noah added in, as if they belonged.

She smiled. "Sounds nice." Rising, she said, "Look at what you've done, Hugo. Everything is beautiful."

He took a breath, easing thoughts of Erin and Noah aside, unexpectedly afraid Jay and Sally might not see it as he did. "My brother and sister loved the original trees and the Santa throne. Maybe changing things isn't a good idea?"

"You think they aren't going to approve?" She laughed. "After everything Sally did to create this place?"

Their gazes connected and he quietly said, "Yes."

She might not see it because she didn't know his entire past.

"I guess if it isn't quite right, we can always change it back next year."

She smiled. "Hey, look at you, being all flexible."

He laughed. That was one of the things he liked about her. Even when the past grabbed him, she lured him to see the future. His long-held beliefs about himself, his life, shivered through him, but they didn't have their usual power. They were weak. Insubstantial.

"I do have my moments when I recognize flexibility helps."

Noah ran over and put his little arms up for Hugo to hold him, and the future leaped to his brain again. Teaching this boy to throw a ball. Helping him with homework. Reading bedtime stories—

Then relaxing in the master bedroom with his mother.

He'd never seen anything so clearly. Never wanted anything so badly. And while his smart, powerful self knew he could bring it about, his cautious side told him there was always trouble lurking somewhere. He'd spent his entire life believing he was made for boardrooms, takeovers and decision-making. How could one woman make him think he'd changed?

They took Noah to the kitchen, and Hugo made a production out of Noah being the taste tester for the gingerbread that would create the enormous gingerbread house centerpiece for the goody table, but also the gingerbread men to be served with vanilla ice cream like sundaes. And, again, the whole experience was so natural, so easy that like a child longing for there to be a real Santa, Hugo could have believed.

But he recognized that was because he *wanted* to believe.

And that's when a man got into trouble. Wanting something, anything, too much was dangerous.

After they returned the office and Erin's mum had taken Noah home, Erin settled into the seat behind her desk. "So? Dinner tonight?"

She might have casually issued the invitation, but there was something in her voice. A hesitation. As if she was as unsure of their situation as he was.

But that was good. It meant she knew as well as he did that their relationship wasn't a sure thing.

He pulled in a breath. "The chef's trying recipes, so we could have anything we want from the menu."

"That sounds perfect."

He heard it again. This time he wouldn't dub

it hesitation. There was more of a professional tone to her voice. Like they were getting together to talk about something pertaining to the hotel, not to make love.

Hugo gave their dinner request to the chef, who, as always, was thrilled to have Hugo tasting the food before guests began arriving the day before Christmas Eve. But as he and Erin rode the elevator to the penthouse, where the chef would deliver their meals, he frowned at her briefcase and coat.

She'd never brought her coat and briefcase up to the room, a blatant reminder that she'd be leaving him alone in the big bed or to go home to his own cold, empty penthouse.

He reminded himself that shouldn't bother him. Even if they really were beginning a relationship, they were in the early stages. Right now, what they were doing was supposed to be casual. Not important. Feeling as if he were bonding with Noah that afternoon, he'd made too much of it. It was time to get them back to the easy relationship they both wanted. If something developed after they returned to Manhattan, that would be great. If it didn't, he would survive. But that was why he wanted this now. Something easy. Something fun.

He walked over, pulled her to him and kissed her. "The chef says we have forty minutes."

She slid her hands to his shoulders. "Oh, yeah?"

"Yeah. Wanna make good use of it?"

She laughed, then kissed him. Long and sweet. The thing he always felt with her stirred in his soul. He took them deeper, delving into her mouth with his tongue, pulling her so close the clothes that separated them didn't matter.

When he broke the kiss, he walked to the bar, retrieving a bottle of wine and two glasses, before he caught her hand and led her back to the bedroom.

They removed their clothes slowly, between kisses that felt different. He knew it was because of his thoughts that afternoon and decided to roll with it. Then he realized she was leading him, her feelings evident in every press of her lips, ever lick of her tongue. Before he could stop it, longing swelled inside him, a need so intense and pure it stole his breath. He couldn't imagine living his life without this, without *her*.

Telling himself to stop thinking that way, he almost swiped control from her. A few shifts, a few touches would have done it. But he liked this feeling. Not a loss of control, but a chance to be himself, let her love him.

His heart stuttered. *Let her love him?*

The thought rippled through him, tiptoed into his brain. She clearly loved him. Nothing was ever as sweetly innocent as the touch of her tongue on his skin, the smooth movement of her palm as it roamed over his flesh, seeking sensitive spots, luring him into the spell she created.

Confused, he lay back, let her explore until the profound perfection of her touch build a fire inside him that would only be assuaged one way. He caught her shoulders and rolled her beneath him, entering her with a thrust that made her gasp.

She'd shown him her curious side. Now he would show her his demanding side. They rode a wave of intense arousal that shattered them. Then she fell asleep at his side and he took a long, slow breath, his heart so soft he knew she held it in the palm of her hand. His soul so open he could feel the fresh air of liberation filling it.

He closed his eyes.

He'd fallen in love and he didn't merely want a life with her. He yearned for it. He wasn't even sure how this had happened. He had a past that told him he wasn't a relationship person. He liked work. He liked success. He liked control.

Nothing that he felt with her was stable or secure. It was fragile and scary and so insubstantial it was almost liquid.

But it was also bliss. Maybe worth more than a sister who didn't like him and a brother who might never really trust him?

Or maybe he'd been right the day before when he realized being with her was so distracting that it might ruin the plan that had been the only thing to keep him sane since his mother asked him to leave?

CHAPTER TWELVE

DINNER——LOBSTER FRA DIAVOLO, flavored with clam juice on cognac——melted in Hugo's mouth. Erin seemed to enjoy hers, but the odd behavior he'd noticed before they'd made love had returned.

She was nervous. Not out of sorts the way she had been the day he'd fed her lobster and filet mignon. But jumpy about something.

His thoughts after making love returned and he realized that whatever they were doing, having fun or falling in love, it snagged all his mental energy and could ruin his plan to get his family back together. Not because she was demanding, but because the feelings he'd had when she made love to him made everything else in the world seem irrelevant.

And his brother and sister could not be irrelevant. His past had to be cleared or he'd live with the shadow of secrets and lies his entire life.

When they finished dessert, she rose from the

table that the wait staff had set up in the sitting room and walked to the chair where she'd left her briefcase.

Conflicting emotions skittered through him. If she left so quickly, so easily, it would confirm that what they were doing was only about sex. Irrelevant. And his focus could return to where it should be. On his plan to fix his family. Clear his name.

But what she had done in that bedroom hadn't felt irrelevant.

He said nothing. Leaning back. Watching her. The feeling in the air confounded him. The mood had shifted from the intense warmth of what they'd just shared to something disjointed and jagged.

"I have something for you."

He still said nothing. The tone of her voice said it wasn't a gift.

"Something I found."

"Found? Where?"

She faced him. "In a box." She winced. "Actually, as I was moving junk out of that corner so I could set up my desk, it fell." She pulled a manila envelope from her briefcase. "This spilled out."

She held it out to him, and he took it, his heart thundering in his chest. Would she have made love to him so sweetly if she'd found the evidence Nick had trumped up to make it appear Hugo had been the one who'd embezzled?

She might. Especially if what he'd believed was profound emotion was her goodbye.

Their gazes held.

She whispered, "Open it."

His emotions a knot of chaos, he poured out the contents of the envelope. Smaller red and green envelopes greeted him. "What's this?"

She swallowed without answering, and curiosity compelled him to look down again at the envelopes—

Addressed to Sally and James.

His gaze leaped to the return address. *His.*

"What the hell?" He glanced up at her, then back at the cards. "I sent these to my brother and sister. And they're—" he peered down again "—not even opened."

"They were all together in the box. As if someone had intercepted them and stashed them away."

"That jerk, Nick!"

She shook her head once, quickly. "Wouldn't you assume Nick would have destroyed them?"

His face fell. "You think my *mother*…kept these from the twins?"

"I think she intercepted them in the mail. Whatever her reasons, she didn't give them to your brother and sister. But I also believe she couldn't throw away the only part of you she still had."

He slammed the handful of cards to the table beside his empty plate. "She didn't have any problem tossing the whole me away. Why keep these?"

She shrugged.

Hugo scrubbed his hand across his mouth, his head spinning, his heart so heavy it hurt to breathe.

Watching myriad emotions race across Hugo's face, Erin held her breath, wanting to understand how he felt and to reconcile the man he was beginning to show her sparingly to the one he showed the world. The guy who'd barely paid a whit of attention to her in two and a half years and now suddenly couldn't keep his hands off her. The guy who'd been sweet and kind to Noah that afternoon. The guy who'd laughed with her.

The guy she was trying not to love but couldn't help herself. He held so many secrets and they hurt him, and she couldn't love another man with secrets. She couldn't let the chance to get answers to her questions pass.

"Hugo, what happened to make you leave? You say your mom tossed you out and she clearly kept these cards from your brother and sister. But she also couldn't throw them away." She spread her hands imploringly. "Every time you tell me about your Christmas Eves, I see the perfect family. What happened?"

He took a breath. "My dad died."

"You didn't leave when your dad died." That much she'd gleaned from the newspaper in his desk drawer.

"No. My dad dying changed everything. He was the engine behind our great Christmas Eves." He ran his hands down his face. "He was the engine behind everything. When he died, our mother couldn't cope. She was a fantastic mum, but Dad was the one with the business sense. I was too young to realize it, but she was failing. When she started dating Nick—he'd been a frequent guest at the hotel—she saw salvation. She married him and essentially let him take over."

"That's…" She almost said *sad*, but remembering her state after Josh died, how hard it was sometimes to simply put one foot in front of the other to get herself to work, she changed her mind. "Actually, Hugo, as a widow myself, it makes sense to me."

"Well, I was a teenage boy who saw it all differently. It felt like a betrayal."

"You gave him a hard time?"

"I tried to get along until things got bad. I

started hearing innuendos in everything he said. Thinly veiled threats to kick us *all* out. The reminder that we'd be homeless, living on the street without him. Especially after Mum gifted the hotel to him as a Christmas present."

Erin gasped. "She gave him the hotel?"

"Yes. It was jaw-dropping. Odd. Everyone thought it was a gift of love, but I had this horrible sense there was more to it. By then I was seventeen, and decently smart because I'd worked at Harrington Park since I was young. My dad had even begun showing me the inner workings like employee schedules and bookkeeping. So I sneaked a peek at the books and realized Nick was cooking them. Money supposedly spent on renovations for Harrington Park was actually being siphoned off and going to his other businesses...most of which were failing. He did this for so long and so consistently that he'd bled Harrington Park dry."

"You left because he was embezzling?"

"No, like a fool, I went to him. Told him what I'd found. Gave him a chance to come clean with my mother." He sniffed a laugh. "That's the enthusiasm of a teenager. Or maybe the naivete. That night my mum called me into the office and confronted me with evidence that showed I was the one siphoning off the money. Nick's money, she'd said, because he was the one who owned the hotel. She wanted to know where it was. I told her that I hadn't taken it, Nick had. But Nick was older, smarter and probably accustomed to hiding his deeds. He bested me at every turn. Even threatened me with arrest. And the ongoing hints were also in there. Suggestions that with the hotel being his, if my mum took my side I wouldn't just go to jail, but she and the twins would be out on the street. The silence was so thick in the room, the click of a pen would have sounded like thunder. Eventually, my mother told me to leave."

"Oh, my God. He framed you!"

"He *used* me. I gave him just enough information and time to turn the tables and, in the process, turn my mother against me."

Erin held out one of the Christmas cards. "She still loved you."

"Right. Keeping a few Christmas cards proves she loved me? I think her not giving them to Jay and Sally proves she didn't." He combed his fingers through his hair. "For a while I toyed with calling the police myself. The real accounting had to be somewhere. All they had to do was find it. But I looked at Nick's face and I knew if I didn't leave, Nick would throw my mother and my brother and sister out into the street. That night. Christmas Eve."

The penthouse fell silent again. Even Erin

could feel the ghosts of Christmas Eves past haunting the quiet room.

She walked to Hugo, putting her hands on his forearms and sliding them up his biceps, but he shrugged her off.

"No," he said, stepping and turning away. "Stop."

She retreated, feeling and seeing the reserved Hugo returning. Not about to let that happen, she said, "I still say she loved you."

He spun to face her. "Oh, really? She never once tried to contact me, and she kept my messages to my brother and sister away from them. How do you get love out of that when it's pretty clear she didn't want me in her life?"

"You yourself said she was under a lot of pressure—"

He remembered that. Remembered her fearful eyes. Remembered how he'd wanted to help her—

Suddenly he was seventeen again. As fearful for his mother as she was for herself. He glanced at the cards. Pictured himself at eighteen, addressing the first ones to Jay and Sally. So hopeful. He'd been that way every year. Choosing just the right cards, penning a personal message, absolutely positive that year would be the year he'd get an answering card or letter.

It was only after his cards began coming back to him marked "addressee unknown" and he knew his brother and sister no longer lived at Harrington Park that he'd stopped sending cards and begun making plans to buy the hotel. He'd known the only way to bring his family back together would be to buy Harrington Park.

And that was working…sort of. Jay was trying. Sally was cool. But she had fashioned the garden. She wanted to be part of the hotel.

She simply didn't want any part of him. For years he hadn't let that hurt him, but these past weeks it had. Because he'd gone soft. Wanting things he'd known all along he couldn't have. He was the strong businessman, older brother. Not their peer. Not someone who begged them to like him.

"Let me help you through this."

He also wasn't a man who let himself be vulnerable. Erin was so beautiful and so loving, it had been tempting to succumb—but he suddenly saw it wasn't right.

It was not who he was—not who he could be if he wanted to bring his family together again.

"I'm fine."

She laughed sadly. "No. You're not."

Anger whipped through him. She wanted him weak? She wanted him humble?

"I'm fine." He didn't care that his voice was

loud, his tone impatient. "In fact, I'm glad my mother didn't show them these cards. I'm not going to show them either. I was a sad, lonely kid, trying to make amends. But Jay and Sally didn't need a friend. They needed the strong big brother who should have protected them. *That's* the family we all want back."

"No. What you want is honesty. Honest relationships."

"No, what *you* want is an honest relationship. Josh hurt you, so you think everybody in your life has to be soft and vulnerable about everything. That's not how some of us are made. Some of us are made to be strong, made to absorb pain and solve problems—"

"Hugo! No!"

His resolve strengthened along with his disappointment in her. How could she not see? Or was being with her the problem?

"Yes. That's who I was made to be." He pulled in a determined breath, feeling like himself as his lungs filled with air and his muscles solidified. "Actually, I think it's time for you to leave."

"Okay. I do need to get home to put Noah to bed."

He shook his head. "No. I think what I'm saying is that you and I need to back off. You're soft and sweet and you see the world a certain way. But I can't be that way."

Her face twisted in confusion. "You're breaking up with me? Over a simple argument?"

"It's not simple for me. This is my family—my *life*. And if you want to split hairs, we never really were together."

She blinked. "It felt like it to me."

"And that's the difference between us. Something always held me back, made me question everything about us. Now I know what it was." He motioned around. "This. I don't want to be soft."

Saying that aloud filled him with certainty. No longer confused or angry, he turned toward the master bedroom and his jacket and phone. "I'll see you in the morning. We have a lot to do to make sure this project is on track…the way it's supposed to be."

CHAPTER THIRTEEN

SEEING HUGO WAS not only serious, he was determined, Erin punched the button for the elevator, confusion making her breath stutter. Those cards had triggered something in him she couldn't quite put her finger on, but he'd changed right before her eyes—

And meant it.

Just as she had feared, she'd landed in the middle not merely of his personal battle, but also of his fight to fix his past and reunite his family.

She raced through the lobby with tears in her eyes, avoiding Ronnie's gaze as he opened the limo door for her, and just barely had herself composed when she walked into her apartment.

"Hey, Erin." Her mom rose from the sofa. "Noah's done nothing but talk nonstop about seeing Santa on Christmas Eve. He's so excited. He even calls Hugo, Ugo."

Halfway through shrugging out of her coat,

Erin stopped dead in her tracks. Hugo's reaction had been unexpected. She knew he was smarting from finding that his mother had kept the cards from Sally and Jay. She'd thought she could talk him through it. But he'd turned back into businessman Hugo so fast she hadn't been able to keep up. And though he hadn't blamed her for what his mother had done, in the heat of the moment he had ended their relationship.

She could think that—maybe—he'd feel differently in the morning. But their romance had happened so fast, they hadn't built any real trust, and at their first problem, he'd pulled away from her.

What he'd really done was yanked himself away—dropped her—so he could go back to being himself. The guy who didn't need anybody. The guy who didn't *want* to need anybody.

Maybe that was the thing that always bothered her about them, the thing that wouldn't quite let either of them believe their relationship would last? He didn't *want* to need anybody because the first people in his life, the people he longed to have in his life, had asked him to leave. And that hadn't merely hurt, it had forged who he was.

He couldn't make a commitment, fall in love, because he was always afraid it would be snatched away. So he'd always hold something back.

No matter how much she loved him, Josh had taught her the pain of living with someone who always held something back.

If he hadn't broken it off, she should have—

They were not right for each other.

The realization that she'd really lost Hugo, permanently this time, stole her breath, filled her eyes with tears. When things between them were good, they were perfect. But life had taught her some hard lessons. Still, no matter how logical, losing him hurt. He might not have loved her, but she had loved him.

She still loved him.

She almost told her mom she was thinking about not attending the Christmas Eve celebration, but there were things she had to do at the hotel the next day.

Forcing a smile for her mom, she said, "Ugo? That's funny." Then she faced Noah. "Okay, little friend, let's get you into bed."

She slid Noah into pajamas and closed her eyes when he gave her a good-night kiss on the cheek.

He pulled back and with a happy grin said, "I love you."

Her eyes filled with tears. Though his coloring was hers, his bone structure and facial features belonged to his father. She'd made peace with Josh, with his death, with his secrets, because Hugo had helped her to understand him.

How could it be that they weren't right for each other—

She didn't need to figure it out. The truth was like a neon sign. She and Hugo did not belong together.

Now she had to figure out how to get through the next few days, especially the Christmas Eve celebration. Then she could go home and try to heal.

Because this hurt. It hurt worse than losing Josh. She felt like a part of her soul was being ripped from her. But how could that be when he'd never really trusted her?

Hugo returned to the first floor to get his laptop so he could do some work in the penthouse that evening. He wasn't going to his London flat. He had to get the celebration back on track. Get his game face on. Whip this hotel into shape so that nothing, not even the color of the smallest ribbon, was wrong.

The elevator opened on the lobby, dressed up in evergreen branches, lights, ornaments. The scent of pine mixing with the smell of fresh paint took him back decades. Every December, his dad had the hotel repainted for the big Christmas Eve celebration.

If he closed his eyes, he could picture it.

He expected a flood of joy. But for the first

time, picturing those old Christmas Eve parties didn't feel right.

He didn't feel right.

He stopped in the center of everything. The perfect recreation of his past shimmered around him.

And he didn't feel right?

He'd put his world back into place after seeing those cards. He'd pulled himself together, more determined than ever to fix his family—

His phone rang. Thinking it might be Erin, he slid it from his pocket to refuse the call, but the caller wasn't Erin. It was Jay.

He clicked to take the call. "Yes?"

"Well, you're in a chipper mood."

Those weird feelings that something was off tumbled through Hugo again.

"No matter. What I have to tell you will cheer you right up. When Sally said she was going home, I assumed Tianlipin. Turns out she meant her flat in Kensington. She's definitely attending the Christmas Eve celebration."

And just like that, the weirdness disappeared. Sally and Jay would both be at the Christmas Eve party.

"That's great."

"Yes," Jay happily replied. "Everything will be perfect."

Hugo started to answer, but the odd feeling

returned. He and Jay had always been eager to work things out, but how could their relationship be real if his brother and sister didn't know a big piece of their family puzzle? That he'd sent them cards and their mum had held them back.

He took a breath and suddenly realized the oddness he'd been feeling was about those cards. He couldn't withhold the knowledge that his mother had kept his Christmas cards from them. He and his siblings needed to talk this out. All of it.

His brother and sister had to know he hadn't deserted them. He didn't really want to paint his mother in a poor light, but maybe he was simply tired of being the bad guy.

He arrived at work the next morning lost in thought. Now that most of the hotel renovations were complete, his staff had gone back to New York to be with their families for Christmas. He'd offered them the chance to attend the celebration, but most had wanted to go home.

He walked through the renovated lobby, beautifully decorated, and the odd feeling he had the night before was gone. Confirming that his decision to show Jay and Sally his Christmas cards was essential to getting the three of them back together as a family.

He glanced at a red ribbon with gold trim and his heart stuttered. He remembered his mother choosing that ribbon, then realized Erin had spotted the detail and recreated it—

His heart swelled with emotion, but he took a breath. It was her job to please him. And it was his job to do this right. Not be soft. Be strong. Be the guy who could hold his family together.

He stepped into his office and stopped short when he saw Erin sitting at the small desk in the corner.

His heart tried to kick-start again, but he remembered his decision the night before. To show his siblings those cards. To set this past right. To not be soft.

To forget the happiness he'd found with her.

To forget the thought that he might be falling in love with her.

To get back to being himself. Hugo Harrington. Smart, savvy, successful.

The last thing he wanted was to compromise who he was.

He considered telling Erin she could go home, to end the weird parade of thoughts he had around her, but practicality wouldn't let him. There were things to be done. Not to mention last-minute disasters. Problems she'd need to handle. Especially if his siblings' reactions were good. Then his party could be the event he'd longed for.

The businessman in him would not let her go home.

He very casually said, "Good morning."

Erin didn't even look up. "Good morning."

Her cool reply went through him like a knife. But he hadn't changed his mind about their relationship. The next day or so would be incredibly awkward. But he deserved it. He'd known better than to start something with her. He hadn't been able to resist temptation.

He shrugged out of his cashmere overcoat. "The lobby is gorgeous."

Her attention focused on whatever she was reading, she said, "I got it as close to the pictures as I could."

"Yes. You did. Thank you."

Then he didn't say anything else.

The room filled with silence, but there was no way around it. He loved her son, might even love *her*...but he couldn't be the guy she needed. He didn't want to be the guy she needed.

Smart, strong Hugo would reunite his family, build hotels all over the globe, rule his world.

Erin blinked back tears and rose from her seat. She reminded herself they weren't right for each other, but it didn't help. She kept seeing him funny and happy, and part of her knew that was the guy he was supposed to be.

The guy he didn't want to be.

"If you need me, I'll be in the ballroom and courtyard garden, checking on a few things."

With that she walked out of the office she'd now be sharing with the guy who'd just shattered her heart.

Guests had begun arriving, filling the lobby with laughter in anticipation of what Hugo had done with his family's hotel. That bolstered her mood a bit as she pulled herself together walking to the ballroom and the courtyard garden.

Hugo's sister had done a remarkable job.

His brother had found the chef.

And Hugo had proof that he'd tried to keep in touch with them, yet all he saw was evidence that his mother hadn't loved him.

She had to work not to sympathize with him. Those cards had broken him, but she couldn't care. No matter how much she wanted to hug him and remind him he was one of the smartest, most wonderful people in the world, she couldn't. Not only did he not want to hear it, but she had to save herself. If she didn't pull away, she might end up not able to get away. In love with a man who wouldn't return her love.

It was unthinkable. Yet somehow her heart

kept drawing her back. And she knew what she had to do.

Sitting on a bench in the serene garden, she pulled out her phone and called her mother. "What would you think about returning to Manhattan for Christmas?"

Her mom groaned. "Erin, all of Noah's gifts are here. We have a tree I'll have to take down. Not to mention packing!"

"Doesn't matter. As long as we can get it all done by Christmas Eve and find a flight for the three of us to go home that day, it'll be fine."

"You don't want to stay for Hugo's big party?"

"No." She almost said Hugo didn't want her to stay for his big party. But that wasn't true. He'd want her around for last-minute problems, and she'd keep seeing the happy man inside him desperate to get out. She couldn't risk getting soft again.

She needed to go home. To think of Harrington Park Hotel as just another job. To be in her own home with her son and her mom. To have a normal Christmas and then throw herself into the work of making sure her clients for New Year's Eve parties were taken care of.

Because if she let herself stop too long, she'd feel the pain in her bleeding heart, and she didn't have the strength for that.

She'd lost enough already in her still-young life, suffered enough. Being widowed, having her son alone, raising her son alone—

She just wanted to go home.

CHAPTER FOURTEEN

KNOWING SALLY WAS in town, Hugo phoned her and requested her presence at the hotel. Then he called Jay and told him the same thing, making it sound like hotel business that needed to be discussed, not something personal.

Aware that Erin was buzzing around, working on last-minute details as if her life depended on it, he shoved down the self-loathing at hurting her by reminding himself it was for the best. One way or another, his family situation would resolve itself over his Christmas cards. He simply wanted it done. So he could go back to being a hotel magnate. Someone who found his sense of purpose by making other people happy.

Refusing to even let himself think about Erin, he waited for his brother and sister in the penthouse. When the doors opened on Jay, he asked him if he'd like some coffee or a drink, and though Jay chose coffee, Hugo poured himself a glass of bourbon.

Sally arrived a few minutes later, glowing and wearing a ring on the third finger of her left hand.

"I see congratulations are in order."

She gleefully said, "Yes!"

Hugo hugged her, his spirit lifting. He'd been a strong big brother when she needed it. He had to continue behaving that way.

Sally and Jay sat on the sofa and Hugo lowered himself to the chair across from them. He picked up the manila envelope from the coffee table and slowly poured out the Christmas cards.

Jay said, "What's this?"

"Christmas cards. Addressed to you and Sally. All are postmarked, which proves I didn't desert you." He met Sally's gaze, then Jay's. "I tried to keep in touch."

Sally glanced at the red and green envelopes, then looked up at Hugo.

Jay rummaged through, finding the cards addressed to him and pulling them out. "There are so many cards here."

"I didn't give up until my cards started being returned by the post office."

Sally murmured, "That was probably when we were sent away to school."

A shaft of pain pierced Hugo's heart. It was no wonder it was so difficult for him to get through to them. They'd been as betrayed as he had been.

Jay laughed nervously. "Do we get to read these?"

Hugo leaned back in his chair. "Yes, but I need you to understand that I was lonely and missing you too. If I sound weak, that's why. But trust me, I'm back to being the big brother you knew. I had a few rough years, but I used them to make myself strong."

Sally quietly said, "You want us to read them now?"

His confidence fully in place, he met Sally's gaze. "No. You can take them home with you, if that would be more comfortable for you."

Having scooped his up, Jay said, "Okay." His smile was warm when he said, "I can't wait."

Hugo laughed. "Remember I was just a kid when I wrote some of those cards."

Jay laughed. "I know. I know. You're back to being big brother Hugo now."

But Sally shook her head. "You think sending us a few cards absolves you of everything?" She took a disgusted breath, squeezing her eyes shut. "All this talk about you being weak? When were you *ever* weak? You seemed pretty strong when you left us! Left our mum. If you truly believed that Nick was so bad, you should have stayed!"

She stormed to the elevator. Because the little car had just brought her up to the penthouse, it opened the minute that she tapped the button. Before Hugo could say anything, she was gone.

But Jay stayed behind. His hand hovered above Sally's cards.

His eyes rose and he caught Hugo's gaze. "You sent us a card every year?"

"Yes. And I didn't leave. I was pushed. Nick fabricated evidence that I'd stolen from the hotel."

"Young as I was, I still remember the whispers about money being missing."

"Nick took it." Hugo sucked in a long breath. As long as Jay listened, he intended to talk. "I'd found the evidence and confronted him. I gave him time to come clean with Mum. I never thought the bastard would use the time to frame me."

"So, you did nothing wrong?"

"I did nothing wrong." Hugo waited a few seconds then said, "Go ahead and take the ones addressed to Sally. She might not want them this very minute, but in a day or so she might have a change of heart." Strong, honest, he smiled at Jay. "You have a better chance of getting her to read them than I would."

After Jay left, Hugo strode to his office, his head swimming. Part of him still couldn't believe his mother hadn't given his Christmas messages to his brother and sister. The pain of it rose again and tried to weaken him but he refused to let it. All those years he'd waited for even a simple acknowledgment of the cards and mourned when he didn't receive so much as a thank-you. But no response had come because his mother hadn't given the twins his cards.

And now Sally wouldn't read hers and was still hurt and angry. Not that he blamed her. She had been a kid, left by her big brother, living in a house filled with tension.

Alone in the office, he looked at the outdated filing cabinets that lined the right wall, fighting back his anger with Nick. Death had taken his father, then grief had stolen his mother. Only a shell of herself, she'd married because she'd needed help, needed a partner. And what had she got? A thief. A thief so clever he'd edged out the only person who really knew him.

The bastard was a liar and a thief who had caused the people in Hugo's life to believe *he* was the thief. The people who should have known him best—

Erin knew him.

The idea tiptoed through his brain as soft as a feather. As real as warm summer rain.

He groaned. Erin was wonderful. But he couldn't have her. He wasn't himself with her—

But he'd liked the guy he had been with her.

The thought entered his brain softly again, as if afraid to form. And he knew why. Ever since he'd bought this hotel he'd been confused, trying to reunite his family and renovate a hotel so old a lesser man might have bulldozed it.

Yet he hadn't been as preoccupied with the hotel as he should have been because he liked being with Erin so much more—

Fury burst like a volcano and he swept his arm along the cluttered top of the row of cabinets, sending papers flying.

Angry with himself for losing control when Erin could walk in any minute, he bent to pick up the debris. He had two armloads of unmitigated junk—stuff so dated it should have been tossed a decade ago—when his gaze fell to an old Harrington Park Hotel manila envelope.

He might have simply stacked it up and thrown it back to the top of the cabinets, except his name was scrawled across the front… *Hugo*.

Could there have been another Hugo associated with the hotel?

Maybe.

But his heart sped up as his curiosity piqued. The envelope was so old…

He rose and took the envelope to the desk. Using a letter opener, he sliced the seam and reached inside for the contents.

Ten cards tumbled out.

The first had his full name and one of his former addresses on it. He scrambled to read the others. Each had his name and one of his addresses.

His mother's name and the hotel information had been scrawled in the return address space of the envelope.

He couldn't breathe. His mother had tried to send him things?

His heart thundered, tightening his chest.

Fear tried to tell him that the contents of those envelopes might not be good. She might have sent him threatening letters, trying to get her money back—

He shook his head, setting aside the fear. It wouldn't matter if they were threatening letters. He already believed his mother hated him. They couldn't do any more damage than that.

But if these were happy letters, Christmas cards, even letters expressing sadness that she hadn't defended him, then he wanted to see.

No. He *needed* to see.

He ripped them open. And read the most wonderful words he had ever seen in his life.

She was desperate.

She was sorry.

She loved him.

He read each card, then read the more memorable ones again and again, his heart lifting with every swipe of his eyes across her broken-hearted words.

He wished for a moment that he could have had confidence enough to see her desperation and that he'd swooped in and rescued his family. But wishes to change the past were fruitless.

And he hadn't been unloved.

He sat back on his seat, the whole situation of his leaving played before him, except differently. He saw his mother's pain, saw her love for him.

Things could not have turned out any differently. As a seventeen-year-old without an education, he couldn't have supported his family. His mother didn't have skills enough to get a job that would pay her enough to support a family.

She'd had to let him go. And he'd done very well by himself.

He straightened in his chair.

He *had* done very well for himself. He'd educated himself, worked his way up the ranks of companies…

He'd created a wonderful life for himself, and now he could make it better by bringing in his brother and sister. Not as the superstrong older brother—

Just as their brother.

A strange relief filled him, along with thoughts of Erin. And Noah and even Marge. They'd never once wanted him to be anything other than what he was. And if his brother and sister wanted him to be something more, a superstrong brother for them to lean on...was that right?

Wasn't the world supposed to be more like the one he and Erin had been creating?

The thought confounded him. Instinctively he knew it was right. But he'd spent his entire life believing otherwise. Believing he had to be tough and focused. Not made for the softness, the comfort, the ease Erin had brought into his life.

And this was his moment of truth.

He pulled his phone from his pocket and texted both Sally and Jay for another meeting, this one in his office.

Each came scurrying in, again thinking there was a crisis with the hotel. Jay immediately took a seat in front of his desk. Sally stopped cold when she looked at him, her distrust so evident he could finally see her pain.

But he'd been gone, out of the family, for seventeen years, and so young when he'd been forced out that he suddenly wondered how any of them could believe any of this was his fault.

Nodding for her to take a seat, he said, "Sally,

I see that all this hurt you. Maybe even more than me. I was seventeen, old enough to plan a future and work my way into it. You were a scared kid."

Looking at her hands, she said nothing.

Hugo took a slow breath and said something he never thought he'd say. "That's why we need each other. Not as me being the white knight older brother who swoops in and fixes everything. I'm not that guy." His shoulders relaxed as he said the words, and the relief that filled him rained down as if straight from heaven. "But I would love to have you both in my life as my brother and sister. Just simple family." He picked up three of the cards, all of which contained heartrending letters from their mum. "These are from Mum. I'm going to leave you two alone to read these, to process everything."

With that he left. If Sally didn't understand after reading their mother's letters, she never would. But at least he could let her go with a clear conscience.

He stepped out of the office, closing the door behind him. Erin approached, frowning. "I have stuff in there I need. I hope you didn't lock it."

He stared at her. If he hadn't spent these past days with her, he would have seen his mother's letters as vindication but still believed he somehow had to be more than he was, more than what Sally and Jay legitimately had a right to expect.

She was the first person in his life to let him be himself.

Love for her poured through him. He was pretty sure he'd loved her from their first night together. He'd simply been alone so long he hadn't recognized it, and when he'd come close to seeing it, his past had filled him with fear.

He took a breath, ready to shout it from the rooftops, but he remembered that he'd hurt her—had broken things off with her—and he knew he'd have to make it up to her.

He might even have to win her back.

Seeing the stern expression on her face, he realized he'd definitely have to win her back. He just wasn't sure how.

So when his mouth opened, he didn't say, "I love you." He said, "Sally and Jay are in there. The door's not locked, but I would ask that you give them at least fifteen minutes of privacy."

"Oh." She frowned. "Something I should know?"

He laughed. "No. The celebration's not going to blow up in your face. I'm not going to melt down. In fact," he said, bending to kiss her cheek, "things are finally on track."

* * *

Erin didn't know if she should be insulted or heartened by Hugo's kiss on her cheek. So she refused to think about it.

The next day—Christmas Eve—with a flight back to New York booked for that evening, Erin rushed to pack her remaining things before she could get her mom and Noah into a taxi to go to the airport.

Noah didn't want to leave. He had it in his head that Santa knew he was in his new house and wouldn't find him. He crossed his arms and sat on the sofa, refusing to move.

Her mom didn't want to leave either.

"I finally feel like I've found my place in the world now that I've connected with my parents' families. If anything, I think we should scrape together the cash to rent this place in January."

Erin's heart hurt. "I hear what you're saying, and I love that you're finding a place in the world." She tossed the shirt she was folding onto the sofa and closed her eyes. "You were right about me and Hugo. We did start something, but he broke up with me the day before yesterday."

Her mom scampered over. "Oh, Erin! I'm so sorry. He's an idiot!"

"He's not an idiot. When I moved into his office, I found some things. Things that more or less gave him a big piece of the puzzle to his past. It made him angry and he told me our relationship had gotten in the way of his plans for his family. As if what we'd shared had been me dragging him away from his purpose."

Tears filled her eyes and her mom hugged her. "You always said he had trouble with feelings."

She sniffed. "That's why I want to leave before the party. How could I stay here, in love with someone who'd dismissed me so easily, once I'd discovered his secrets?" She pulled in a breath, all the feelings she'd been suppressing suddenly pouring out of her. "What is it about me that no one trusts me? That no one wants to share their secrets and dreams with me?"

"Oh, honey, that's not it. You might have found some things about Hugo's past. But you've told me a hundred times the man didn't have feelings."

He did have feelings.

Erin had seen them. She'd watched him go from being a man so careful that even his hellos were guarded to someone who let her take the lead in bed. There was something there. Something strong and precious. But he didn't want to be that guy. He wanted to hold back part of himself.

The way Josh had.

Even if Hugo wanted her back, that was the

real bottom line. He might be nothing like Josh, but they had a few similar beliefs. Beliefs she couldn't live with.

Her mom heaved herself up from the sofa. "Come on. Let's pack."

"What about your relatives?"

"I can just as easily save some money to come back next summer." She winced. "It'll mean you'll have to find day care for Noah."

"Not a problem," she said automatically because that was her thing. Just as Hugo could be cold and distant, businesslike when pain overwhelmed him, she became accommodating, not letting anyone see her hurt, upset or confusion.

Maybe it was time for that to stop. Maybe she was tired of being the one everybody counted on. Tired of being the one who always did the right thing.

And maybe that was the lesson in losing her husband. It was time to stand up for herself.

Her phone pinged with a text.

Where are you? I can't find you. Someone said they thought you'd left.

Hugo.

He was probably looking for her because he'd decided he wanted more icing on the ginger-

bread cookies…or no icing…or more flowers…
or fewer flowers. A detail that shouldn't matter.
But he was a fussbudget.

She debated not answering him.

But no matter what she decided about herself
personally, he was still her boss. Her employer.
She would do her duty.

I'm at home. We're packing to leave.

Leave? You're not coming to the party?

She took a second. She'd spent the past weeks
working her butt off to make this the perfect
Christmas Eve. Part of her had envisioned Noah
chitchatting with Santa. Her mom had bought a
beautiful party dress. She'd used Hugo's shopper again to get a wonderful red velvet dress to
wear. But every time she pictured herself at the
celebration of Hugo's greatest success, she saw
him coolly greeting her, then shipping her and
her family to a far corner. Because they weren't
anybody. The family of a subcontractor. Not even
an employee.

No.

Erin! You have to come!

Not really. We're homesick. Eager to be in our own space.

For ten minutes there was no reply.
Then…

I'm sending the limo to bring you to the hotel. After that, if you still want to leave, Ronnie will drive you all to the airport.

She almost politely refused but realized very businesslike Hugo had made her a proposition she couldn't refuse. An easy limo ride to the airport? Rather than a cab when she wasn't even sure all her suitcases would fit in the trunk?

Okay.

Her little family was completely packed when Ronnie showed up at her door.

"I've been instructed to leave your mum and son. After you assist Hugo, we'll come back and get them."

"We have to leave for the airport by three."

Ronnie nodded. "Then we'd best be going."

He took her directly to the Harrington Park lobby doors and dropped her off. A light snow began to fall as she ducked under the portico and into the hotel that bustled with the activity of newly arrived guests.

Her heart swelled. These were the people she'd created Hugo's vision for. Parents who had brought their kids all those years ago were now grandparents with adult children and little ones tucked at their sides.

She skirted the long check-in line and headed to the office, but one of the registration clerks stopped her. "Mr. Harrington is in the penthouse. He instructed me to tell you to go up."

She sighed. Surely to God he didn't want her to decorate the penthouse for some sort of private party for business associates?

Annoyed, she rode the elevator to the penthouse, only to have the doors open on a fully decorated sitting room. Holly and fir branches hung over doors. Christmas lights edged the kitchen island. A decorated tree stood in front of the wall of windows, half hiding the view of London.

She looked around in awe. "What's this? Are you having a party up here later?"

He handed her a glass of champagne. "I thought Noah might like it. Especially if he stays over tonight."

"We're not coming to the Christmas Eve party. We'll be over the Atlantic and in our own beds in a few hours."

He set his glass on the kitchen island. "Look, I know I handled everything poorly."

"You did a great job of getting this hotel renovated and the perfect party planned. And you know it."

He winced. "Reverting back to our business relationship?"

"You've said it yourself. You're my biggest client."

"I'm also the guy who loves you."

Her gaze jumped to his.

"I felt it that day. The day you found the envelopes. It didn't sneak up on me. It sort of whooshed through me when we were making love. But I lost it, or maybe it confused me, when you showed me those cards."

"I shouldn't have. They were none of my business."

"They were definitely your business. But the pain of my past had to be dealt with first." He paused, peeked over at her. "I found a second batch of cards. Same place you probably found the first batch. These were from my mum to me." He paused again, then quietly said, "She vindicated me."

Everything she thought about him, this meeting, her own feelings of hurt, fell out of her head. "She vindicated you?"

"Yes. She believed me. She believed Nick had

bled Harrington Park dry. She knew she'd made a mistake giving it to him and a worse mistake asking me to leave. But he'd scared the hell out of her. I got the feeling she was the victim of emotional abuse."

"Oh, Hugo."

"I know. I also know that I was too young to have seen it. And in my last conversation with Jay and Sally, I told them it was time we had a normal relationship. Not some trumped up thing where I'm their knight in shining armor."

"I'm so sorry."

"Jay and Sally are fine. More settled than I am. They don't need a domineering big brother to fix everything for them. They just need a big brother who loves them." He took a breath. "I think my family has suffered enough and it's time for us to let go. I'm going to tell Jay and Sally that tonight."

Erin whispered, "I think you're right." Not only because she agreed with him but because he was telling her—first—before he told Jay and Sally. Confiding in her. Warmth pooled in her heart. Her head cleared. Everything that had happened in the past two days disappeared and her feelings for Hugo rose and bloomed.

"I love you, you know." He ran his hand through his hair. "I'm not sure how that happened. I was so broken that I'd spent over a decade believing I was a stoic businessman who wasn't meant for love. It was easier to believe that than to deal with the possibility that I'd failed and couldn't get my family back together again. Turns out, I don't have all the responsibility. Some of it is up to Jay and Sally."

"I'm so sorry you had to go through all this, Hugo."

"You have nothing to be sorry for. I'm grateful we fell in love despite the mess my life was in." He laughed and held out his arms to her. "I'm so sorry you got caught in the middle of all this."

She'd realized it would happen. She'd known that she'd become part of him dealing with a messy past. She'd tried to prepare for it. But suddenly it didn't matter. She raced into his arms, let him pull her against his solid chest, and breathed in the feeling of being loved, being wanted, being trusted.

"Nothing like that will ever happen again."

"I certainly hope not. Losing your dad, your mom struggling, a thief coming into your life... that's too much for a family to go through twice."

"Agreed."

He glanced down at her and she looked up at him. Both smiled, and then Hugo laughed. "I can't believe I found you."

"I was always there. Right under your nose."

He frowned. "Really?"

"I had the biggest crush on you."

"You didn't!"

"I did. You should have seen the fantasies I created about us."

"You'll have to tell me some day when we have time."

"Or maybe we could recreate one or two."

He laughed, then kissed her. She rose on tiptoe to kiss him fully, and he held her against him so tightly he knew he'd never let her go.

That thought reminded him of the ring in his jacket pocket, and he broke the kiss. Without any word of explanation, he reached for it as he got down on one knee.

"I think it's time we make it official." He opened the ring box, displaying the three-carat diamond solitaire.

Her eyes widened. "Oh, Hugo!"

"Will you marry me?"

"But we haven't known each other long enough to—"

He slid the ring on her finger. "To what? Fall in love? We both know we did. And we both know we've gone through a lifetime of experiences these past two weeks. Enough that we can be sure." He smiled at her. "Say yes."

She pressed her lips together to hold back a flood of emotion, then said, "Yes! Yes! A thousand times yes."

He rose and took her into his arms, kissing her until their kisses turned hot and steamy and he pulled away. "Bedroom?"

"Yes. But first, we have to call my mom. She's undoubtedly got her coat on and is standing by a mountain of luggage."

"We could send Ronnie over there to get them, luggage and all. Then we could come up here after the Christmas Eve celebration and have Christmas morning together...all of us watching Noah open his gifts."

She kissed him. "It sounds perfect."

It did to Hugo too. His brother and sister would always be in his life, but Erin was the woman with whom he'd make a family.

EPILOGUE

THE DOUBLE DOORS to the courtyard garden were pulled apart and Hugo took a breath. "Ready?"

Erin glanced at the stunning garden. He could see her taking in the fir trees and winterberry shrubs. The skating rink was rimmed with lights and would be opened for skating the following day.

She smiled up at Hugo. Her red velvet gown fit her curves to perfection. The white boa-like trim around the sweetheart neckline gave just the slightest peek at the swell of her breasts. The diamond shimmering at her throat winked at him. His Christmas gift to her.

His heart constricted. He'd spent years wanting only to reconnect with his brother and sister. Though his parents had modeled real love for him, somehow that hadn't registered in his brain enough for him to realize that was what he really needed. Someone who cared for him on a level he could neither define nor describe, but a place in his heart so deep and so pure it lifted his soul.

"As ready as I'll ever be."

He took her hand, the diamond on her ring finger nestled against his palm, and he smiled. She was his. And he was hers. They'd never be alone again.

The doormen at the entry sent a signal to the band, which abruptly stopped playing. The MC scrambled to the stage, taking the mic.

"May I introduce the third of the Harrington siblings, Hugo Harrington, and his fiancée, Erin Hunter."

The crowd parted as they walked to the stage. Familiar faces of people who'd attended the original Harrington Park Christmas Eve celebrations smiled at him. There were new faces too. Not new people. The children who'd accompanied their parents to the magical wonderland of Harrington Park Hotel were now adults, attending with *their* kids.

He accepted congratulations and a few handshakes as he walked to the stage and stopped at the mic. Erin stood by his side.

"This was my father's dream," he began quietly. "He'd made that dream a reality for many years before his life ended too soon. We mourned his loss and eventually the loss of our legacy, but we have it back now. And we intend to make every Christmas Eve the highlight of our lives. Thank you all for coming."

He and Erin left the stage to thunderous applause and the ringing laughter of children. He scanned the crowd and found Erin's mum with Noah, standing by the tree waiting for them.

He'd never realized how much he wanted children, but looking at the elaborate celebration with Christmas gifts piled high under the tree, an entire table of Christmas treats and an upcoming visit from Santa, he longed to be a father. Not just to Erin's son—soon to be his son—but to a few new children.

They walked over to the grove of fir trees where Sally and Jay awaited them.

Jay laughed. "Nothing like a grand entrance."

"This is a grand hotel," Hugo said, unable to stop the smile that rose like the sun in the spring. "It deserved a grand reopening." He looked from Sally to Jay. "Ready?"

Jay reached for the ornament with his name on it, but Sally put her hand on Hugo's forearm. "Not quite." She glanced down, then caught Hugo's gaze again. "I need to apologize."

Hugo brushed that off. "No. Sally. Really. All that's over. We start fresh tonight."

"Yes. I agree. But there are some things that need to be said. I was duped by our stepfather. Mother was too. It didn't take me years to figure it out, but it did take until now for me to realize how much he hurt you. Saying I'm sorry doesn't change things. But I think it's a step we all need in order to be able to put the past behind us."

Hugo's breath caught. He hadn't realized how much he'd yearned for someone to say that. "Thank you." Not wanting to linger on the past, he lifted his ornament. "Now, let's officially start over."

Agreeing, Sally smiled. She picked up her ornament. Jay had his.

Hugo faced the audience. "Every year, my siblings and I would place a new ornament on the tree. The idea was that eventually family ornaments would replace all those red and green balls," he said, pointing to the simple red and green ornaments. "Tonight, we pick up that tradition where it left off."

As they turned to place their ornaments on the tree, someone in the crowd cried, "Hear! Hear!"

Waiters in tuxes and white gloves brought out trays of champagne. When they reached Hugo, Jay and Sally, each took a flute, Jay handing his to his fiancée, Chloe, and Sally handing hers to Prince Edward Chen, the love of her life. Hugo handed his to Erin and all three commandeered another flute—Sally's filled with orange juice because of her pregnancy.

"To Harrington Park!" Hugo shouted, raising his glass.

The crowd echoed, "To Harrington Park!"

With the toasts made, the crowd dispersed. Hugo had instructed the band to take a ten-minute break. As parents led children to the goody table that lined the far wall or over to the tree to peruse the gifts, he turned to Sally and Jay.

"There is one more thing."

About to take Sally's hand, tall, sophisticated Edward stepped back. One of Chloe's eyebrows rose. Hugo wasn't sure what the betrotheds of his siblings were expecting of this night, so rather than have their nerves frazzle, he quickly reached into his pocket.

He pulled out two envelopes and handed them to Jay and Sally. "I'd like you to be joint owners in the hotel with me."

Sally gasped.

A quick burst of laughter came from Jay. "Are you kidding?"

"This hotel was all of our legacy. It's about family. It belongs to all of us. Not just me."

Sally murmured, "I don't know what to say."

"I think you said it before." Before she knew he would be giving her one third of the hotel. She hadn't apologized because he'd given her fair share to her. She'd done that out of truth and love.

His gaze met Sally's and she smiled.

They really were getting a chance to start over. As family.

He reached over and slid his arm around Erin's waist. "Besides, I'm going to be a little busy."

Erin laughed. "He's taking me to see all of his hotels."

"And Noah," Hugo agreed, taking Erin's son from Marge's arms. The little boy grinned at him.

"While I spend some time with my relatives," Marge said with a laugh. "I love Ireland and feel like I'm home."

"I feel the same way about Tianlipin," Sally said.

"Which makes me and Chloe the official family nomads." Jay laughed.

"And that means we're going to have to divide the responsibilities for running the hotel."

Jay said, "All three of us? I thought you'd want to run it."

Erin smiled. "Hugo and I *have* decided to move to London."

Jay gasped. "That's great!"

"But I own a lot of other hotels," Hugo said. "That's why we all have to help with the Christmas Eve celebration. All promise to attend."

Sally shook her head at Hugo. "As if we'd miss it."

Jay raised his glass for another toast. "We're a family again."

Warmth flooded Hugo. He had his siblings back, a fiancée, a little boy and a soon-to-be mother-in-law, and he was returning to London. Returning to the person he was supposed to be all along. A little wiser. A lot more compassionate. And very happy.

His life could not be better.

* * * * *

If you missed the previous stories in the Christmas at the Harrington Park Hotel trilogy, then check out

Christmas Reunion in Paris
by Liz Fielding
Their Royal Baby Gift
by Kandy Shepherd

If you enjoyed this story, check out these other great reads from Susan Meier

Hired by the Unexpected Billionaire
The Bodyguard and the Heiress
Cinderella's Billion-Dollar Christmas

All available now!